CHAPTER ONE

S am continued to wipe the hair from her face as it fell with every bump in the road. She was increasingly agitated with each bounce of her dad's old Bronco. The Ponderosa forests of North Central Arizona were particularly stunning this time of year; the snowmelt made everything glisten, and small blooms pushed through the cracks of the pavement. With her head buried in her phone, the beauty of the surroundings passed by unnoticed.

Jack peeked at his daughter with a side-eye and shook his head. *Kids these days and their technology*, he thought. The irony didn't escape him as he glanced in the rearview mirror at his own mound of gizmos and gadgets, stockpiled over the years in his hunt for the unknown.

Jack was a bit of a monster hunter. You might say it was his life's work. In his world, there was no bigger prize than proof that Bigfoots existed. His unwilling accomplice on this venture was skeptical; a realist. Living in a digitized world where new conspiracy theories abounded daily, she chose to

believe that the Bigfoot 'myths' were nothing more than folklore designed to scare kids like her into obeying their parents' whims. Whims like her dad bringing her on this trip . . . hence her underwhelming attitude.

"Promise it's only for one week this time?" she quipped.

"I promise, Princess. I just need to take some soil samples and grab the memory cards from the remote cameras, do a little scouting, and then we'll be on our way."

Sam sulked, knowing trips like this could go on for months, and one week could easily turn into two or three. This time was different, though. In the past, her mother had always kept her company once they went out of range of the cell phone towers. It had been eighteen months since Nan passed. Not unexpectedly, but that didn't make it any less painful. She had been sick for a long time, but Sam's mom had been her best friend, the only person she felt understood her. Nan was missed and needed.

Oddly enough, Sam's mother hadn't been as skeptical as her daughter when it came to her husband's obsession. The influence of the internet and instant access to every question and answer conceivable, had made the young lady a disbeliever of all things magical and special in the world. She could still hear her mother's voice tell her, "It's only make believe if you don't believe."

Sam wanted to believe, but years of endless trips into the wilderness in search of Bigfoot had jaded her. That she lost her mother at such a tender age only helped to confirm that there was nothing special about this big blue hunk of

rock hurtling through space. *We are all just a happy accident.*

Twelve going on twenty. Sam had been forced to grow up too fast, and Jack missed his carefree little girl. Her brownish-red locks bouncing off her shoulders as she chased butterflies through the forests. So inquisitive. So naive and pure. He blamed himself and his never-ending search; a lack of any hard evidence only salting his daughter's doubts. Time after time, he came up empty and left another trip disappointed. Each time, he saw that glimpse of something magical drain further from her eyes. Once his wife passed, there was no trace of his little rapscallion. He knew that if he could prove to her that Bigfoot was real, then maybe he'd see that spark again. Jack knew that if it didn't happen soon, his search for the missing link would result in losing her to the world.

"Are we there yet, Dad?" The familiar moan of a road-weary child went in one ear and out the other as Jack drove on in silence. All he could think about was getting to his field cameras. Checking the footage from the auto-cued surveillance was Jack's drug. He would sit in his study for hours, reviewing every little (or big) creature that showed up in the lens feed. Black-headed Grosbeak. Violet-green Swallow. Red-breasted Sapsucker. More often than not, it was birds tripping the camera's sensors. He had become quite the avian aficionado and often joked with Nan that he should give up on Bigfoot and go to work at The Audubon Society. Of course, he also got hours of entertainment watching the squirrels and raccoons practicing their best selfie close-ups.

Still, that elusive eight-foot-tall beast had yet to make an appearance.

Despite years of research and fieldwork that turned up mostly empty, Nan was always encouraging of her husband's passion and his belief that something extraordinary resided in those woods. It was that unbound enthusiasm that had made her fall in love with the slender blonde fella who sat in front of her in a class she was auditing during freshman year at The University of Washington. Anthropology 113: Myths of America. Nan spent most of her first semester in college auditing classes, still unsure of what she wanted to be when she grew up. Little had she known then, that class was the spark that lit Jack's intense fire. She allowed herself to get caught up in the adventure with him. Every weekend they would comb different areas of the local forests, following leads from years of research forged by his predecessors.

Jack's passion led him straight to post-grad school and eventually, a doctorate in cryptozoology. Shortly after graduation, they married. For the next couple of years, Jack and Nan lived throughout the wilderness of Washington, Oregon, and Northern California. Based on his doctoral thesis, Jack earned a five-year grant to continue his research into the Bigfoot myth. *Myth.* Jack was never a fan of that word. It had a negative connotation in his line of work. Myths weren't real; they were just folklore and fairy tales with no possible root in truth. It wasn't a matter of *if* he'd find a Sasquatch, but *when.*

Nan never stopped believing in him, but three years

into their search they received news that would change their world forever. Nan was pregnant. Although disappointed that he couldn't finish what he started, Jack always put his wife first. She needed him more than ever with a baby on the way, and Jack nestled comfortably into family life. He would take a position as a professor at the university, and although not in the field anymore, he knew he could shape the minds of future believers from the classroom. His work would have to continue through his students and the assignments he would give them. Grad students researched various leads and collected artifacts from the field. Professor Owsian would use their field notes to update his research, giving full credit to his students and the work they accomplished in his name.

Although the pace of his efforts slowed considerably, he was thrilled to become a father. He couldn't wait to share his life's work with his baby girl. She was born into it. Her nursery overflowed with plush Bigfoot stuffed animals and a library dedicated to the subject that he had collected throughout the years. He wanted her to read every one, hoping she'd share his excitement for it all. He'd start slow, however, with his favorite children's tale, *Big Heart*—the story of a little girl who found and saved a young Sasquatch from ill-willed opportunists looking to turn a profit and sensationalize her discovery. Jack and Nan named their daughter after the brave little girl in that book: Samantha.

After Nan passed, Jack understandably struggled to stay focused on his research. The forests he once loved to explore were now a painful reminder of his beloved. Trips without Nan became tedious and no longer joyful, and he refused to bring Sam since her mother's death. It wasn't until Sam started getting into trouble at school that Jack realized something had to change, not only in him, but for the benefit of his daughter. His presence, or lack thereof, meant that he was ignoring the needs of his little girl. He decided a change of scenery was needed, so they packed up and headed to Arizona.

Not considered a "hotbed" of Bigfoot activity by most standards, Arizona had its very own version of Sasquatch, known as the Mogollon Monster. Local legend was that the creature lived throughout the dense forests of the northern and central parts of the state. Sightings were reported as far north as the Grand Canyon, with most clustered around a large area of the Coconino and Tonto National Forests known as the Mogollon Rim. Jack was interested in exploring those areas and set up home in Sedona to be centrally located. Known for its beautiful red rock formations and magical properties, Jack hoped Sedona would help Sam break out of her funk and finally begin to heal.

As Jack pulled the old jalopy to a slow stop, rusty brakes screeched and caused a ruckus of wildlife to scatter. As Sam got out of the vehicle, she noticed the sunlight shining through the forest trees and the games the shadows played. Despite her reticence, she could feel the magic of this place, and it brought her comfort. The wind was whistling through the tall Ponderosas, the leaves dancing across the forest floor.

She was at peace, taking in her surroundings and forgetting about the digital world, even leaving her phone behind in the truck without a second thought.

"Princess?"

"Yeah, Dad?" Sam was already wandering and exploring.

"Stay within shouting distance, please. I shouldn't be more than an hour; then I want to get camp set up, and I'll need your help." Jack didn't hear a reply. "Sam?"

Her response was unintelligible, but it was enough to let Jack know she had heard and understood his request. Jack was growing used to the grunts, groans, and moans of the modern teenager. Was this what he had to look forward to for the next several years? *Teenagers*, he thought, shaking his head. He couldn't help cracking a smile, knowing that she was still a great kid at heart, despite this rough patch.

CHAPTER TWO

S am was in a world of her own exploring the dense forest. Every rock, every leaf, every little bug was a thing of wonder. Soon she had a pocketful of samples she could add to her ever-growing "heart" collection. Over the years, Sam had collected hundreds of heart-shaped items, all made by Mother Nature and serendipitously placed in her path, but none more special than the rock her mom had given her on their first trip together. Sam kept it on her, always. It was a hobby her mother had started with her, and every new item found was a reminder that helped keep Nan's memory alive.

As she continued her hunt, Sam wandered much farther than her dad would have been comfortable with, and stumbled upon a clearing in the forest, flanked by enormous pine trees and what must have been a ten-ton boulder. Upon examining the rock, she noticed a heart-shaped divot. She traced it with her finger, wishing she could show her mom.

Suddenly, a heavy breeze picked up. Leaves began

swirling on the forest floor, dancing with the ebb and flow of the winds; it was mesmerizing. Sam was in a trance, watching as streams of leaves twirled, rising through the trees. She was in disbelief as five separate funnels formed around her, spinning to the treetops almost two hundred feet high, her hair blowing in all directions. Sam wasn't scared, though perhaps she should have been. It was magical! Then, as suddenly as it started, the winds stopped. Calm. Quiet. It was eerie after the chaos from moments before. Sam was uneasy now. *What was that?*

She gathered herself, fixed her tousled hair, and began looking around. Fear was setting in. She heard a loud snap from behind her and turned, but saw nothing except for the massive boulder which had been there all along. Not wanting to find out what had made the noise, Sam high-tailed it back to the campsite. She couldn't wait to tell her dad what happened. Maybe he'd go back with her to investigate. Maybe he wouldn't believe her. Perhaps she was just letting nature play games with her head.

As she rushed through the trees back into the camp clearing, she shouted for Jack.

"Whoa, whoa, whoa. What's going on? What's wrong?"

Nearly out of breath, Sam tried spitting it out. "Dad, you won't believe what . . ." Her words trailed off as she noticed they were no longer alone. Not wanting to embarrass herself in front of strangers, she quickly went silent. Peering around Jack, she saw a man and three boys. She recognized the man, but couldn't place him.

"Honey, you remember Mr. Stevens, right?" Jack could see the puzzled look in her eyes. "Charlie is my good friend from university in Washington. It's been a few years since you saw him last. It was at your mom's 33rd birthday . . . party." He realized too late that he might be bringing up a painful memory for his daughter. That party was the last birthday where Nan was in full health. Only weeks later, she'd gotten the grim diagnosis.

Holding back tears, Sam choked on her words. "Yeah, Dad, I remember Charlie. Sure. Sorry, I was just . . ." She looked back at the area from which she had just run screaming, ready to tell her dad what she'd experienced.

Thankfully, Jack interrupted her. "Sam, these are Charlie's boys: Chris, Tommy, and Eli. Say hello."

Sam raised her hand meekly and mumbled a barely audible greeting. "Hi."

The boys were relatively close in age: Chris, the oldest, was 16; Tommy, 13; and Eli, 9. Not that Sam cared much. Boys . . . *yuck!* Although Tommy did have soft, brown eyes and a friendly smile. She was instantly disgusted with herself for even noticing those things about him.

Sam was fortuitously sidetracked from her fright by the presence of their new campmates. She gave her dad a disapproving glare; he had not been forthcoming that they'd be having company. She wasn't fond of their presence, as she had been looking forward to spending time by herself.

Charlie and Jack had met during college. They shared the drive to uncover the unknown. Charlie's vice was

extraterrestrial, however. Every few years, the two would get together to help each other with their work, typically out in the field. The last time out, Jack was supposed to go to Peru with Charlie to study the massive Nazca geoglyphs thought to be created by an alien lifeform. It had been the topic of the day at Nan's birthday party, but Charlie ultimately made that trip alone.

"Wow, this place is beautiful, Jack! I can see why you chose to make your way down south. Those Sedona rock formations are a sight to behold. I envy you, my friend. Much better than the cold, wet northwest."

"Agreed, Charlie. I just hope we can start making headway on our research. I checked all the cameras before you arrived, and we have plenty of data to comb through."

Sam glared at Jack. She agreed that Arizona was beautiful, but it wasn't home. She hadn't had a chance to make new friends yet. She was lonely, and still felt somewhat at arm's length from Jack.

"Dad, can I go look for firewood?" All she wanted was to get away from everyone and continue exploring, perhaps go back to the boulder and resume her investigation. She was feeling a bit braver, realizing that maybe she'd overacted to what happened. It was just a windstorm. She was tired, and her eyes must have been playing tricks on her.

"There's plenty of wood right here," Jack quipped, pointing to several branches surrounding the campsite.

"But I saw some really good pieces just past a large rock over there."

"We could use your help here, unloading and setting up the tents, Princess."

"I think us boys can handle this, Jack." Charlie locked eyes with Sam and nodded. He knew what she had gone through and was hoping to befriend her. He also knew that Jack was having a hell of a time trying to find his way as a single parent. Jack was exhausted. Charlie could see it in his face.

Sam wryly smiled at Charlie, appreciating his help. *Perhaps this guy's not too bad after all.*

"Tommy can go with you and help," Charlie added at the last second.

On second thought . . .

"But Dad, I . . ." Tommy chimed in his objection, but was quickly interrupted by Jack.

"Excellent idea. Besides, with two of you, you'll be able to carry more wood. Take the wagons and try to be back before dusk." Jack and Charlie had so much equipment that they would regularly bring heavy-duty wagons with large-tread tires to haul their load more easily.

Sam and Tommy stared disapproving daggers at their dads, but they each grabbed a wagon and set off. "It's this way," Sam said, motioning with her head. She was unhappy about her new companion, but undeterred from returning to her analysis of the boulder and what she'd experienced. Sam didn't say anything to Tommy about it; she wouldn't say anything to him at all. Her silence would speak volumes about her disinterest in him tagging along.

As they meandered through the trees and out of earshot of the rest of the group, Tommy spoke up. "So, your dad seems nice." He tried making small talk to open up a line of communication, but could tell his presence was unwanted. Sam shrugged her silent response. Counting in his head along the way, Tommy waited another hundred steps before trying again. "Do you like Arizona?" More silence.

As they approached the area where the boulder was, Sam slowed, then stopped to look around before entering the clearing between the trees. The wheels on the wagon creaked to a stop. Five large piles of leaves lay on the forest floor in approximation to the wind funnels she had seen earlier. Sam stepped cautiously, once again spooked, but she wouldn't dare show fear in front of a boy. Tommy started to speak up again, but Sam shushed him. A verbal response! It was progress, as far as Tommy was concerned, but he was still unsure of what was happening and why she had stopped.

"Sam? What are we doing?" he whispered. He didn't know why, but he felt whispering was appropriate. *What's this girl looking for? Did she hear something?* Tommy was growing uneasy with every passing moment they stood there.

Sam dropped the handle of the wagon and moved toward the boulder. She could hear something barely audible on the other side, but couldn't quite make it out. Her hands started to tremble as she reached the boulder and placed them on the granite slab . . . *it's warm!* Sam turned toward Tommy. He could sense she was finally about to speak to him, but just as the words began to form on her lips, a ferocious wind picked up, stronger than the one before. Piles of leaves swirled around them chaotically.

Tommy, scared, screamed out, "Sam! Sam!"

Her reply was lost; she could only return a desperate look of panic. Seeing this, Tommy rushed to her side and grabbed her hand. He pulled her behind him, fighting the fierce winds to ensure they were beyond the clearing and far away from the boulder. They shielded their faces from flying leaves and twigs with their free arms. The gale was so strong that dirt, small rocks, and even tiny branches joined the leaves. They were pelted mercilessly.

Then, it happened. An intense flash of warm white light encompassed the forest around them. They quickly closed their eyes, but it blinded them nonetheless. Sam and Tommy ducked behind a tree for cover, holding each other tight with their heads buried in each other's arms. Just as fast as the episode had started, everything went silent. No wind. No light. Nothing.

Slowly, the two pulled their heads from their protective hovel and made eye contact. Sam was shaking. Tommy instinctively held her tighter to try and make her feel safe, but Sam quickly pulled away. She wanted nothing of being so close to someone she just met, regardless of whatever it was they had just experienced. They jumped to their feet, faces red from both fright and embarrassment, and perhaps a bit flush from being so close. Sam didn't want to think about that. She played it off and once again showed her indifference. Tommy stood there, staring at her.

"Stop," she requested. But Tommy couldn't remove his gaze. "What are you looking at?"

Tommy finally realized he was gawking at her and deflected. "Nothing. Just making sure you're okay. What was that?"

They began to brush the leaves from their hair and dust off their pants. "Not sure," Sam said shortly. Despite everything, she still wasn't interested in conversing with him.

Sam started to move back toward the clearing, to see if there was a clue of what had happened. This was the second time and she still had no idea what was going on. Tommy was right behind her, staying as close as possible in case of a repeat performance by Mother Nature.

Sam stopped suddenly in the middle of the clearing, spinning around quickly to check her surroundings. Tommy wasn't prepared for such an abrupt halt. Their faces were inches apart. When their eyes once again locked, they each turned the same shade of red they were blushing moments earlier. Tommy reached up and pulled a leaf from Sam's hair. Startled, she jumped back and moved as quickly as possible out of his reach, scowling at him, incredulous at his brazen action.

"Please don't follow me like that," she snapped.

"Sorry, I was just trying to keep up. Didn't realize you were gonna stop so fast."

"And do not touch me again." She flipped her hair, turned away from him, and started back toward the giant rock when she caught herself smirking. What were these

thoughts going through her head? *No boys!* Pushing them out of her mind, Sam continued to the boulder. She tentatively placed her hand on the same spot as before.

"What are you doing?" Tommy asked.

Sam's eyes got big. "It's cold."

"Shouldn't it be?"

"No, you don't understand, it was warm. When I put my hand here before, right before the windstorm, this rock was warm . . . hot, even."

"Well, maybe the wind cooled it down?" It seemed a reasonable explanation, and he was only trying to help. Tommy walked toward the boulder so he could feel for himself when a swirl of wind started moving the leaves around again.

Sam turned toward him. "Run!" She whipped past him. Tommy quickly turned tail and followed her, not waiting to to be left behind. They did not look back and did not stop again until they reached camp.

CHAPTER THREE

S am and Tommy emerged from the path and into camp completely winded, struggling to get words out to describe the bizarre episode near the boulder. The others, still trying to get their temporary living facilities set up, dropped everything and rushed to their sides. "What's going on? What's wrong? Where are the wagons?" Jack rattled off. But they were still trying to catch their breath.

Sam finally took a long, deep breath and gathered her thoughts. "You didn't see that?

"See what, Princess?"

She was unconvinced that no one else had seen or heard anything. "The wind. The light. Everything!"

Charlie jumped in, "What are you talking about? Tommy, what happened?" Even though Sam failed to give any real details, she felt like she was being doubted—at least by Charlie.

"You didn't see the bright light? It practically blinded us! And that wind?" Tommy asked.

"We didn't see anything. And the wind has been pretty calm all day. Just how far did you go?" Charlie asked, his initial worry fading in favor of annoyance. "Tommy, I'm not in the mood for any games. Is this some kind of joke?"

Sam jumped in, "Dad, we swear. It's what I was trying to tell you earlier, when I came back the first time. Something strange is going on. The wind keeps picking up in a clearing just down that path. But it's not normal. The leaves swirl into huge columns, rising all the way to the treetops."

Charlie, disbelieving, responded sarcastically, "It's just a wind vortex. Nothing special, sweetheart. Happens all the time in nature. I think you two are letting your imaginations get the best of you."

Sam shot a look that could've melted Charlie where he stood. Jack saw it and jumped in. "That's strange. It wasn't windy here at all, other than a light breeze. What about this light? Where did it come from?"

"I don't know. It was everywhere. It was so bright we had to cover our eyes." Sam glanced at Tommy, remembering being huddled closely with him. Tommy simply smiled.

"It's starting to get dark. Let's finish setting up camp, and we'll check it out first thing in the morning. Deal?" Jack knew not to be dismissive of his daughter. It had taken a long time after Nan passed to start gaining Sam's trust and understanding, and he didn't want to compromise his progress in any way. Sam nodded in approval. "Now, can you and Tommy collect some firewood from around the camp, please?"

Without a word, they started gathering twigs and branches and piling them up near the center of the camp, all the while steering clear of one another. Perhaps it was Sam who was keeping her distance, as every time Tommy would try and work his way toward her, she'd move in the opposite direction. Sam sensed this was puppy love just getting started, but she'd fight it as long as she could. *Let the games begin.*

As night drew in, with the temperature dipping, everyone bundled up. With camp finally put together, Sam and Jack started to gather food for dinner while Tommy arranged their chairs around the firepit. Chris helped his dad start the fire while Eli looked on. The growing flames and hunger pangs pulled everyone close.

Eli was captivated by the dancing flames, and Chris took notice. "Eli." No response. Louder still, "Eli." Still no response. The boy's gaze was fixated; he seemed almost frozen. Chris reached out and grabbed Eli by the shoulder to break him from his trance. "Eli!"

"The birds," he responded, still half dazed.

"What are you talking about?"

Eli snapped out of it. "The flames. They look like birds flying out of the fire. Don't you see it?"

"The only thing I see is an overactive imagination. Get it together, bro."

"At least I have an imagination, butthead!" They all started to laugh. It was contagious, and even Sam managed a mild chuckle despite the serious thoughts consuming her about what had happened. The forest would have been quiet that night, if not for their raucous behavior.

Once the laughter died down, they went about preparing their meals. Three cast iron skillets sat atop the fire, one full of precut veggies softening in butter, another filled with bacon baked beans (Sam's favorite), and the last sizzling with hamburger steaks. They were eating like royalty. Sam had always complained about her dad's campout meals. Jack could just as easily survive on trail mix and beef jerky, and there were plenty of times Sam had to as well, but not this time. Mealtime by the fire had just gotten a lot more fun, and Sam was famished.

As everyone finished their last bites, Eli ran off and started fumbling through the supplies. Chris shook his head and smiled wide, knowing what he was searching for . . . *s'mores.* What's a camping trip without a treat, after all? "Sam, would you like a . . ."

She cut Chris off, "Phoenix."

"I was gonna say s'mores."

"No . . . what Eli saw in the fire. The firebird. It's called a phoenix." She turned to Jack, who gave an approving smile. His daughter was well versed in mythology, as she should be, having sat through hours of his lectures. Typically it was Bigfoot, of course, and occasionally extraterrestrials, but the myth of the phoenix was one she'd heard throughout her childhood. It was her mother's favorite.

"Don't tell Dad," Nan would whisper to Sam. "We wouldn't want him to think we don't like Bigfoot, after all." They would giggle quietly, not wanting to alert Jack to their secret.

"Ok, but what's that have to do with s'mores?" Chris questioned. "Focus, young padawan."

Tommy let out a snort at the Star Wars reference, assured that Sam had no idea what Chris was talking about, but when he caught Sam's eyes, he immediately felt his face redden and burn. He didn't want her to think he was making fun at her expense.

Sam shot right back at Chris without pause, "Ok, Jar Jar, would yousa likesa an explanation?" Tommy laughed again, even harder, but this time at Chris. Sam's impression was spot-on. "Laugh it up, fuzzball," she quipped at Tommy. The boys were both impressed, but Tommy was in love; she really knew her Star Wars.

"Shoot, kid; I'm all ears," he replied. Chris couldn't contain his smile despite the put-down.

Everyone stopped to listen to Sam recount the legend of the phoenix. "It's a mythical immortal bird that lives in Paradise which enters the mortal realm every thousand years, to build its funeral pyre. On the following morning, when the sunlight breaks over the nest, the bird stretches out its gold and red feathers and sings a hauntingly beautiful melody. At that moment, the nest catches fire and burns to a pile of ash, leaving behind only a small worm. Three days later, from the ashes, the worm morphs, and the phoenix is reborn to breathe new life. It will return to Paradise and not return for another thousand years, when it will repeat the process again. The story of the phoenix teaches about life, about growing and learning from mistakes, about never giving up, and about healing. It is believed that the tears of a phoenix can heal human suffering and give life."

Jack looked on with great pride, getting teary-eyed. He secretly knew all along that this story was a special bond Sam had held with her mother. He was also cautiously optimistic that she might follow in his own footsteps. Perhaps one day he could pass the torch and Sam would continue his life's work, maybe even find Bigfoot if he couldn't. *A dad could dream, right?*

"Extraordinary, Sam. Jack, you taught her well." Although Charlie was impressed, Sam was not a fan of his. She still felt stung by what she had seen as condescension earlier. She couldn't wait until morning, to show them exactly what she and Tommy had seen.

With the fire flickering and the howls and yips of coyotes in the distance, the group settled in for their first night under the stars, slipping into their canvas abodes. Ever-hungry Eli snuck a baggie full of popcorn into his tent for a midnight snack, dropping a trail behind him that was immediately noticed by Charlie. He shook his head in admiration of his young son's hearty appetite.

Sam and Jack were the last to turn in. "Goodnight, Princess. Thank you for sharing that story with everyone. You'd have made your mother proud. That was always her

favorite."

"You knew?"

"Always. Your mother was the most amazing woman I've ever known, and you are every bit her daughter. I love you, honey. Goodnight."

"I love you too, Dad," Sam said with a wide grin. She started to walk toward her tent, but suddenly couldn't help herself. She turned and ran into Jack's arms, hugging him harder than she had in a long time. "Goodnight."

CHAPTER FOUR

I t was still mostly dark outside. Sam rustled in her sleeping bag, prying open one eye to see if it was morning yet. *Morning.* She sat bolt upright and quietly opened the flap of her tent. Looking around, Sam took in the sights and sounds. The racket from the crickets was palpable, though their familiar chirp was waning fast, replaced with the faint songs of the forest birds. Daybreak painted the low edge of the sky in soft pinks and oranges. Directly above, the twinkle of the night sky was beginning to dissolve into a familiar blue.

Looking around the campsite, Sam realized no one else was awake yet, but her desire to show her dad the boulder was growing urgent. She unzipped her tent fully and took a step into the dewy air. Stretching her arms, Sam let out a prolonged yawn complete with sound effects, but no signs of consciousness materialized. She moved herself closer to her dad's tent, replaying her yawn even louder this time. Rustling could be heard. *Maybe one more yawn for good measure.*

"Sam, are you up already?" Jack asked groggily.

Her hangdog response gave Jack his answer. "Who, me?"

"Well, if your name is Sam, then yes, you." He opened his tent. "Isn't it a bit early yet?"

"I know. I'm just anxious to go back and show you the rock. I want you to believe me! I want you to see for yourself!"

"Shhh. Keep your voice down; I don't want to wake the others. I tell you what, let's get dressed and we can head down there now. Just the two of us."

Sam cherished the idea of showing her dad without anyone else tagging along. She knew Tommy could corroborate her story, but that meant Charlie would be there as well, doubting every word from her mouth. Sam jumped back into her tent and got dressed in record time. Jack wished she was this eager on school mornings.

Father and daughter made their way quietly, tip-toeing until they reached the tree line, turning back to ensure they hadn't woken anyone. Assured they were clear to proceed alone, Sam picked up the pace. It wasn't long before Jack was wheezing. "Whoa, Princess, slow down a bit. Your old man isn't as spry as he used to be."

Sam turned and gave him a big smile, refusing to slow down. "Come on, Dad, keep up."

"Just how far is it? I thought you said it was 'just down the path.'"

After twenty minutes of hiking, they approached the clearing. Sam slowed and turned to Jack, concerned. "What do we do if it happens again?"

"Don't worry, I came prepared." Jack reached into his knapsack and pulled out one of his remote cameras. He looked around, being careful not to enter the clearing. He could see the massive boulder Sam had mentioned on the other side. Massive was an understatement; it was easily twenty feet wide and ten feet tall. Jack pulled a strap from his sack and tied the camera to one of the trees, focusing it directly on the giant granite slab. He popped in a new SIM card, and looked for Sam's approval. With a quick nod from his daughter, he powered on the camera and started recording.

They stepped into the center of the clearing and slowly took in their surroundings. Jack looked up, stunned by the massive height of the evergreens. The trees must have been hundreds of years old. If the Mogollon Monster lived around here, they would make great scratching posts. Jack started examining the tree bark for signs of animal hair.

Sam quickly made her way over to the rock. "Dad, come here." She was forgetting that her dad got side-tracked all too easily. "Dad!"

"Huh? Oh, sorry. I was just . . . uh, never mind." Jack, somewhat embarrassed, made his way over to Sam.

"Feel the boulder, Dad."

Jack laid his hand on the giant rock, and his eyes doubled in size. *It IS warm.* He looked at Sam in disbelief. Sam

had turned around, expecting a fierce wind to pick up at any moment, but all remained calm. She placed her hand on the rock again, trying to tempt Mother Nature to reveal herself. Still, nothing.

"I don't understand. Last time, both times, as soon as I placed my hand on the rock, that's when it happened. The wind and the leaves." She was disappointed despite the fear of experiencing the force again. Turning back to the rock, she found the heart-shaped divot and, as she had before, traced her fingers along its rough, bumpy form. Then, it happened.

Slowly, the forest floor began swirling. Sam was frightened at the prospect of another storm and clutched her dad's side for protection. The wind picked up ever so slightly as five vertical columns of leaves formed and rose skyward. No storm. No violence. Just leaf funnels dancing up through the trees. Jack could not believe what he was witnessing. It wasn't that he had doubted his daughter, but what she had described had been hard to understand until now. They both began laughing in amazement of what was happening.

Just as soon as it started, it was over, and the leaves came to rest in five large piles in the center of the clearing. Jack looked at Sam, still unsure of what had just transpired. "See Dad, I told you I wasn't crazy!"

"No, Princess, I never thought you were, just that maybe your imagination was getting the best of you. But this . . . wow. I, I don't know what to say."

Sam turned back to feel the rock again; Jack followed suit. It was still warm. "The heart. I think it has something to do with the heart," she said.

Jack started to trace his finger over the heart, and once again, the winds began to swirl. He immediately lifted his finger and everything calmed. He was speechless. Sam, wanting to try and recreate the magic yet again, started to reach her finger out, but Jack stopped her. "Wait. Not again. Not yet."

Jack slowly made his way around to the other side of the boulder. It was partially buried into a small berm, forcing him to climb up one side, using the stone to brace himself. *Still warm on this side,* he noted to himself. As he reached the backside of the rock, he saw what appeared to be a hollow dug out from under the rock; something had created a den. The opening was about three feet wide and rather narrow, disappearing deep underneath. Not wanting to wake whatever might be in there, Jack backed up slightly and called Sam to join him. Things were slowly starting to make sense. The rock was warm because whatever creature was living in there was causing a transfer of heat to its surroundings. *It would take a gigantic creature,* he conjectured, *and yet the opening is slim.*

As Sam made her way around the giant mass, Jack reached back into his sack and pulled out a flashlight. Slowly, he kneeled and flickered the light into the cavern. It was empty save for some twigs and branches, and what appeared to be the makings of an unfinished nest. Moving in for closer inspection, Jack noted that the space widened, forming a ten-foot-wide by eight-foot-tall burrow. He could feel an unusual amount of warmth emanating from the cave, seemingly too warm for any normal forest creature.

Suddenly, his eyes widened. *Wait, could this* be *it?! Bigfoot! The Mogollon Monster!* He turned to Sam, "Princess, we may have finally found it!"

"Dad, are you sure?" Sam was doubtful, but realized it wouldn't be fair to her dad, recalling what it felt like when her discovery was questioned.

"I mean, we don't know one hundred percent, but this may just be the biggest clue yet! Come here." He led her by the arm, hurriedly pulling her back to the other side of the rock. He pointed at the heart.

"Wait," she replied skeptically. "Are you saying what I think you're saying? Dad, I love you so much, but . . . Big Heart? You know that's just a book, right?"

"Touch the heart again, Sam," Jack demanded in excitement.

Sam did as he asked, and the winds slowly picked up. She removed her finger rather quickly, scared now that they might be in the presence of a giant, hairy storybook character. "Dad, can we go back to camp, please? We should probably let the boys know about this." Despite her reticence around Charlie, Sam knew he could help her dad piece together the puzzle better than she could. Besides, there was strength in numbers, and she wasn't willing to wait around to see who, or what, would be coming home. "Please. You have your camera recording everything. Can we just go?"

Jack was beside himself. "Yes, Princess, let's go get

some more supplies and bring everyone back here to investigate further. This is unreal!"

Not wanting to waste time or get caught falling behind, Sam rushed past her dad and back onto the path eastward, toward camp. *I can't wait to tell Tommy about this!*

She caught herself in that thought, and squashed it.

CHAPTER FIVE

S am blasted her way into camp, expecting that by now everyone else would be up. All was quiet, but not for long. Her exuberance quickly caused the others to stir. "What is going on out there?" Charlie called from inside his tent, clearly agitated at being woken so suddenly.

"We found something," Sam shouted. "Under the rock! On the rock!"

The boys all peeked their heads from their tents, confused and half-awake. "What are you talking about, Sam?" Tommy asked.

Before she could answer, Charlie chimed in, "And where's Jack? Where's your dad?"

At that moment, Jack emerged, stumbling in from the trees. He leaned over and grabbed his knees, attempting to catch his breath. "Thanks for waiting, Princess," he said sarcastically. "Charlie, you have to see this. Grab your gear. We need to set up more cameras. Grab the thermal scanner, too."

"I'm hungry, can we have breakfast first?" whined Eli, always thinking with his stomach.

Charlie took the opportunity to razz his boy. "What, the popcorn in your tent wasn't enough?'

"I have no idea what you're talking about, Dad,"

"Mhmm, must've been one of those sly forest creatures that left that trail all the way to your tent." Charlie noticed that most of the popcorn from the previous night was no longer there. "I'm guessing you had a little help last night," he continued, pointing to the remaining kernels.

Eli disappeared back into his tent and quickly cried out, "Hey, who stole my popcorn?"

"Eating in your sleep again, bro?" shouted Chris.

"No, I swear. I was going to eat it, but I never did and the bag is gone." Eli was perplexed.

"Alright, enough of this tomfoolery," Charlie chided. "Jack, what's going on?"

"We don't have a moment to lose. This may finally be it."

"The Mogollon Monster? You found evidence?"

"A den. Whatever lives in there is quite large, so large that the boulder was warm from the transfer of body heat. I can't think of another creature that could create that type of heat. Not even a bear. Can you?"

The camp was now buzzing with excitement as the boys gathered all the equipment they could carry. Sam appointed herself the defacto chief, ensuring everyone was moving faster than they wanted to so they could get back to

the rock right away. Charlie landed several blows with his eyes at Sam, annoyed by her hurried persistence. Sam shot right back, letting him know that she wasn't going to be intimidated. This discovery was bigger than him; it was bigger than any of them. "Let's go!!" she yelled, staring right at Charlie. "We're losing daylight."

Chris, moving faster than he wanted to, couldn't help himself. "Pretty bossy for such a young one."

"Not now! Get moving!" she barked.

Jack looked over at Sam, proud and yet frightened by his daughter's gravitas. *Just like her mother, not taking guff from anyone.* He couldn't hide his smile. That feisty spirit was what he loved most about his wife. It brought him a sense of peace, knowing that Sam would be the same strong woman.

Eli made sure to grab a handful of leftover marshmallows and graham crackers so he wouldn't starve. As he grabbed everything he needed from inside his tent, a rustling against the backside startled him. The shadow of a creature with big ears and an unusually long tail scampered away, scared by Eli's frightful refrain. He scrambled as fast as he could, not ready to meet what he believed was the popcorn thief, and zipped his tent up tight so nothing could get in while they were gone.

Sam was still fired up and trying to get everyone going. "Five minutes, everyone! Meet at the path when you're ready, so we can double-check that we have everything. Hurry!"

"Jack, that girl of yours is something else. Very . . . assertive."

"Thanks, Charlie. She is something special," Jack replied, feeling that Charlie's perfunctory comments were less than flattering.

The group began to gather at the trailhead, checking their gear and preparing for the all-day outing. Chris was pulling up the rear, still fumbling to pull his rucksack over his shoulders. "Anyone have any food?" he said, staring at Eli, who was stuffing his cheeks with the marshmallows. An apple came flying from the center of the group toward Chris' head. He speared it at the last moment with one hand, just in front of his face. He nodded and smirked at Sam. "Thanks." She nodded in return.

Tommy, witnessing this exchange, glared at his big brother in jealousy. "Can we get going now?" he said, clearly annoyed.

"Right behind you, bro. Lead the way," Chris retorted.

Tommy took the opportunity to try and establish some power. He had an advantage over his older sibling, having been to the boulder before. He jumped ahead of Sam on the pathway. "This way. Let's go."

Trying to get everyone up and out of camp was a bigger ordeal than Sam had anticipated. She was happy to let her guard down and allow Tommy to lead.

As the group approached the clearing, Sam sensed something was amiss but she couldn't figure it out. There was a

briskness to the air she hadn't felt the other times she was here. It was colder, denser. Sam ran up to the boulder and immediately felt it . . . *cold*. But not the same cold from when she and Tommy were there the day before. It felt nearly frozen. She quickly traced her finger over the heart in the rock. *Nothing*. She turned back to the clearing, bewildered by what she was seeing . . . or more precisely, what she wasn't seeing.

Jack could sense her anxiety setting in. "Sam, what is it?"

Charlie was bringing up the rear of the group and had just stepped into the clearing. "Move! Everyone move!" Sam demanded.

Charlie snapped at her. "Sweetheart, you need to calm down."

Jack looked at Charlie in disapproval. He was thrilled that Sam was excited about this—about anything. "Move back, like she asked," Jack requested sternly. "What do you see, Princess?"

Everyone backed away from the center of the clearing; everyone except Charlie, who planted himself firmly in the center of the action. Sam wanted to say something, but was afraid of the trouble she'd be in if she were to say what was on her mind. Seeing she was about to snap, Jack put his hand on her shoulder to calm her.

"The rock is ice cold. Tommy, feel it. You know what it felt like yesterday." Tommy made his way to the rock without hesitation.

"It's freezing! I don't get it. Yesterday it was warm and

then it got cold, but not like this."

"Trace the heart, Tommy," she commanded. Charlie looked on in comic disbelief as his son snapped to her orders. Nothing happened. "And look," Sam continued, pointing to the leaves in the clearing. "The leaves. No piles. They're just everywhere."

Unimpressed and growing weary of the child's allegory, Charlie chimed in. "So we have a cold rock and leaves on the forest floor. It looks like a great place to camp if you ask me," he surmised with a sarcastic laugh. "Jack, a little help here? I'd like to hear from the Bigfoot expert in the group if you don't mind." The animosity between Charlie and Sam was growing more tense. Everyone could feel it.

Jack gave Sam a look, which she immediately understood; she needed to stay calm and let him handle things. "Earlier, that giant boulder was warm to the touch, unusually warm considering what time in the morning it was. The sun wasn't even coming through the trees yet." Jack walked up to the rock and pointed. "And here. This heart-shaped carving right here." Jack moved back to the center of the clearing, trying to get everything out. "And there were five piles of leaves here. When we traced the heart with our fingers, the winds picked up and the leaves started swirling into perfect columns that reached the tops of the trees."

Charlie couldn't help but smile in jest of this fish story. "Really, Jack? This is the story you're sticking to? You expect me to believe that? So the rock was warm, then it was cold, then warm again, there were dancing piles of leaves, and now the rock is frozen. Did I get that right?" He looked right at Sam and shook his head.

In her most snarky, disdainful voice, Sam replied, "Yes, you got that right, Charlie." Now things were getting serious—a child calling an adult by their first name. Chris, Tommy, and Eli's mouths were on the ground on hearing Sam's retort to their dad.

"Charlie, step down," Jack admonished his friend in defense of Sam. "Considering the field we're in, you should be the last one cajoling anyone for a discovery of this magnitude."

"A discovery? This all sounds like fantasy. Magic. Hocus-pocus."

Sam quickly jumped in. "Oh, but aliens and Bigfoot are normal?"

"There's a difference between cryptozoology and fairy tales of magical heart-shaped rocks, darling. There's proof, however limited, of Bigfoot's existence." Jack felt Charlie's passive-aggressive dig. "There's proof and documentation of alien lifeforms visiting this planet."

"You want proof? Let's check the camera," Jack suggested. "We caught it all on film." Jack removed the camera's SIM card, but realized it would require his laptop, which he had left behind. "Once we get back, I'll be happy to provide your proof."

"What you are proposing is make-believe, regardless of what's on that card."

At the risk of sounding childish, Sam couldn't help

replying the way her mother would. "It's only make-believe if you don't believe. I believe!" Charlie dropped his head and chuckled.

Jack jumped again to his daughter's defense. "So do I, Sam. Now excuse me, Charlie. My daughter and I have work to do."

Charlie's newfound temperament astonished Jack. He had always been even-keeled, friendly and caring. It was a side of his best friend he had seen once before, but thankfully never since. Jack chalked it up to the news he'd received from Charlie just prior to the trip—he and Nelly were getting divorced. She couldn't take anymore of his alien-chasing adventures, leaving him to his true passion. The boys were not yet aware.

Jack made his way to the backside of the boulder to reinvestigate the opening and den. Sam followed close behind, trying to stay as far as possible from Charlie. Tommy tagged along as well, despite Charlie's disbelief in their story. Although not the direct recipient of his father's ire, the verbal attack on Sam might as well have been aimed at him too. His dad didn't believe and clearly had no desire to.

Chris looked at his dad. "Now what?"

"I'm heading back. If you boys want to stay here chasing fairies, then be my guest." Charlie grabbed his pack and started back toward camp with Eli following, not wanting to catch his dad's anger. Chris paused, looking at the rock, then back at his father. He dropped his head in contemplation. Chris had no reason to doubt Sam and Jack,

but he decided to make his way back to camp as well, if for nothing else than to keep Eli company.

Jack yelled out to Charlie as he faded into the forest. "Can you leave the thermal scanner, please?" No response. Jack, Sam, and Tommy sat there in silence for a moment, staring at each other and reflecting on what had just happened. "Let's get to work," said Jack, as he started rifling through his gear. "It's gonna be a long day."

CHAPTER SIX

Charlie stormed into camp with Chris and Eli on his heels. He set his pack down and immediately began rifling through his tent in search of something. Chris and Eli looked on in confusion. Charlie's head was clouded, and he didn't know what to do with himself.

"Dad?" Chris asked daringly. Charlie continued, unfettered. Chris, unsure he had been heard, spoke up louder. "Dad, do you need help with something?"

Charlie's answer was unintelligible. It was clear that they should just stay out of sight until he had a chance to cool down. The boys made their way to the opposite side of the camp and kept their distance.

"I'm scared," Eli shared.

"I know, me too. I've never seen Dad like this. I think we just need to lay low right now and not say anything that'll get him any madder, especially at us."

Eli was anxious. "We're just gonna sit here and wait?"

Doing his best to put his brother at ease, Chris decided

to keep Eli occupied. "Grab the football. Let's toss it around for a little bit."

Eli fetched the ball and began throwing it back and forth with Chris, careful not to make too much noise. But it took less than a minute for Eli to grow impatient and break the silence. Careful to stay out of earshot of his dad, Eli's curiosity was abundant. "What do you think they saw back there? Could it really be Bigfoot?"

"I'm not sure, bro. Whatever it is sure has everyone spun up, especially . . ." Chris nodded toward Charlie's tent. "Hopefully, they can figure it out."

"Do you believe what they were saying about the leaves?"

"I'm not sure what to believe at this point. I mean, I suppose if Bigfoot and aliens are real, then what's to say there isn't some sort of magic heart-shaped rock that makes the wind blow?"

"Well, I believe, but please don't tell Dad." Chris nodded. Eli was worried about how Charlie would react to this knowledge. Tommy was left behind, and he didn't want the same to happen to him.

Charlie was a good father. He would do anything for his boys. Before this bizarre morning, he had never given them reason to think he was anything but a loving, doting parent. Seeing him like this was scary; they didn't know what to do. The knowledge of the impending divorce may have provided some explanation, but Charlie wanted to protect them as long as he could. Eli looked to Chris for guidance, but even he was unsure of what would or should happen next. For now, it seemed best to stay quiet and out of their dad's way.

The brothers continued to toss the football, but something pulled Eli's attention—something moving near his tent that he spotted out of the corner of his eye. "Chris," he whispered. "Look."

"What is that thing?" Chris asked. Sniffing around the tent was Eli's popcorn thief—a raccoon-cat-weasel hybrid of some sort. It had big, dark eyes surrounded by a white furry mask, large perky ears, and a tail as long as its body with black rings running the entire length. It perked its head up at being discovered, and stoically stared back at the boys.

"I remember learning about those in scouts. It's a ring-tail cat," Eli answered. "It's not really a cat, though. It's more like a raccoon."

Bending down on one knee and removing a grape from his pocket, Eli attempted to lure the animal near, clicking his tongue. The sleek creature tentatively moved closer to examine the offer. "It's ok, you can have it," Eli coaxed. Soon the little cat was within reaching distance, sniffing Eli's hand before snatching its bounty and darting back to safety.

"Looks like you've got yourself a snack buddy, bro." Chris laughed as the creature retreated out of sight.

Eli rolled his eyes. "Just throw the ball, butthead."

In an attempt to show off his arm strength and athletic prowess, Chris overthrew Eli. The ball bounded its way across camp and hit the side of Charlie's tent before coming to rest. Charlie immediately stopped what he was doing, threw open the flap, and emerged with a scowl. Chris and Eli looked at each other, unsure of the fury that was about to be unleashed.

"Sorry, Dad. My fault. I was just trying to show Eli how to throw a perfect spiral." Chris would do anything to protect his brother.

"Get over here right now," Charlie demanded. Both boys scurried at the command. Looking at Chris, "I want you to go back to the boulder. I want you to see what's going on there. Do you understand me? Report back to me everything you see and hear." Chris nodded in compliance.

"Me too?" Eli asked.

"Only Chris! You're staying here and helping me. Now go!" Chris wasted no time grabbing his sack and heading out on the trail toward the others. He looked back briefly, worried about Eli.

Once out of sight of the camp, Chris stopped to take in the events of the day so far. He was still shocked by his dad's reaction, and his assertion that everything Sam, Jack, and Tommy experienced was nonsense. Chris was not as wide-eyed as young Eli; he was still skeptical. He wanted to believe, but like his dad, he needed more proof. He wanted to see what was on the footage Jack had filmed. Taking his pack off his shoulder, he placed it on the ground and loosened the drawstring, keeping the contents inside. There it was, right on top, the thermal scanner.

With Charlie distracted and more focused on his rage

than anything else, Chris had grabbed his dad's pack instead of his own. They looked similar. Same brand, same army green color, but Charlie's was a little more used and grungy. Chris trusted his dad wouldn't notice, given his current state. Chris remembered that Jack had asked Charlie to leave the scanner. Despite his own doubts, and wanting nothing more than for his dad to believe, Chris hoped Jack would be able to prove his claims. Maybe then Charlie would see that this wasn't some elaborate hoax. Of course, he was scared of what might happen if it were all true.

Chris cinched up the pack and kept moving, picking up his pace to try and get there as soon as possible. As he made his way down the path and through the trees, he got lost in thought. *There has to be a scientific explanation.* His dad had taught him that everything is understandable through science.

"Myths and folklore are just things that science has yet to verify. Stories are handed down through generations, crafted in truth, but not yet proven to be true," Charlie would often lecture. "The science itself required to make these discoveries may not even be real yet." The profoundness of his dad's musings kept Chris intrigued and wondering what future scientific discoveries could bring.

As he replayed the memories in his head, the irony of his dad's current state of mind started to dawn on him. *This could be the scientific discovery of a lifetime. A real Bigfoot! How could he not believe?* Chris realized that perhaps, just maybe, he did believe. The revelation stirred something in him, and he felt himself running full speed to get to the rock and help with the investigation.

In his zeal to help, Chris sprinted through the trees, but suddenly came to an abrupt halt. Not knowing what hit him, he found himself face down on the ground, short of breath with a mouthful of dirt. Still dazed, he looked behind him in search of answers, and sticking out of the earth was his foe—the horizontal root of one of the surrounding trees. Chris rolled back onto his stomach, accepting the cold, wet forest floor soaking through the front of his now-ripped shirt, the warmth of the sun on his back making it bearable.

As he gathered himself and regained his breath, he realized that he was no longer in possession of the backpack and its precious cargo. Propping himself up on one elbow, he spied the sack behind him, where it had come to rest against a tree. Finally feeling a bit better and ready to continue, Chris propped himself up onto his hands and knees and drew in a deep breath. Staring at the ground, he realized that the warmth enveloping him couldn't be the sun. He was in the shadow of the trees.

Jumping to his feet, Chris spun around to take in his surroundings. In an instant, the shadow below him disappeared and the shade of the forest was pierced with bright sunlight. As he craned his neck to see what was above, the overhead sun blinded him. He averted his gaze to regain his vision. Holding a hand above his brow to form a makeshift visor, he looked up once again. Nothing was there except the treetops and the sun shining directly on him, but it had now become noticeably colder, even though the shadows of the trees were at least twenty feet from where he stood.

"What the . . ." he said aloud to himself, short on words. "What was that?" He continued to look around in all directions, up and down and through the trees. Nothing revealed itself; not a single clue. Attempting to make sense of things, Chris tried telling himself it was just a large bird flying by. *But birds don't hover. Do they? I was in that shadow for at least a full minute.*

Realizing he was in the shadow of a massive unknown something that gave off a lot of heat, his thoughts immediately turned to his dad's work. *Aliens? Could that have been an extraterrestrial ship? Was I just abducted?!* Chris, now duly frightened, grabbed his pack, turned, and continued running toward the rock. He knew he had to share this with the group.

Within minutes, Chris busted through the trees into the clearing and immediately noticed five perfect piles of leaves, just as Sam had described earlier. "Guys?" Chris called, not sure where the others were. He walked backwards across the clearing, keeping the leaves in his sight, not daring to look away. He continued cautiously, unsure what he was seeing.

"Over here," Sam responded from behind the boulder.

Chris made his way to the backside of the rock, placing

a hand on the giant slab to help himself over the berm. Despite his focus on the piles of leaves, the coldness of the stone on his hand stole his attention. It was still chilly, but not as icy as it had been earlier.

"Where's Tommy?" Chris asked.

Tommy popped his head out from the hole under the rock, revealing a smirking, dirt-smudged face to his brother. Only Sam and Tommy were small enough to fit through the narrow opening to the cave. Wanting to show his bravado, Tommy had quickly volunteered before Sam could edge him out.

"Chris, check this out." Tommy was eager to show his older brother what they had been learning. Chris swung the pack off his shoulder and slowly lowered himself onto his stomach to peer inside the opening. Jack noticed the dirty, ripped shirt Chris was donning and the spooked look on his face.

"Son, are you okay? It looks like you've been in a tussle. Where are your dad and Eli?"

Staring into the deep well below the rock and looking around with the help of Tommy's flashlight, Chris answered, "They're back at camp." He was unsure what he was supposed to be seeing. Tommy was just getting ready to explain, but Chris sat up, attempted to dust off his shirt, and turned to Jack. "Dad is pretty mad. I don't get it. He wanted me to see what you guys are doing. I probably wasn't supposed to tell you that, though," he said shamefully.

"It's ok, Chris. We haven't found much yet, but we're

just getting started. So far, all we're seeing is the nest in there. There's some residual heat coming from the branches and twigs. Here, look at this." Jack handed Chris some small stones, which appeared to be charred. "These were inside the nest. There's also some slight scorching on the nest and the underside of the rock."

"So, there was a fire under there?"

Sam, wanting to show off her investigative prowess, chimed in. "Well, yes and no. If there were a big fire under there, the whole place would be black with soot and ash. All the wood would have completely burned."

Jack continued, "It's tough to tell what's going on here. There's no sign of animal life. I'd expect to see fur or the remains of prey, but there's nothing. The heat signature doesn't seem to make much sense either, especially given what we felt earlier when the whole rock was warm."

The revelation by Jack sparked Chris' memory. *The thermal scanner.* He immediately grabbed his pack, yanked on the drawstring to loosen the opening. He reached in and pulled out the scanner, handing it to Jack. "I thought you might need this." Chris explained how he had grabbed his dad's pack when told to spy on them, and that he hoped they would find evidence that could prove to Charlie their story was real.

"Sam, get in there with Tommy. I'm going to hand you the scanner," Jack instructed. Sam had spent most of her childhood playing with her dad's equipment out of boredom, especially on trips like these.

"You know how to use that thing?" Tommy asked. Sam shot him a wry smile as she flipped the switch to the device.

Chris, meanwhile, was curious about the leaves. "When did that happen?" he inquired, motioning to the piles of leaves.

"We don't know," Jack replied. "We were so engrossed over here that we never noticed. The wind never picked up or anything. One minute it looked like you saw it this morning, and the next there were five perfectly formed piles. Lots of puzzles to solve here. I wish your dad were here to help out."

"Not to add to your workload, sir, but there's something else." Chris regaled them with his "UFO" encounter. Sam and Tommy stopped what they were doing to climb out of the hovel and listen.

Something spectacular was undoubtedly going on in this forest, something magical and other-worldly. Sam was no longer the doubting, jaded little girl. She believed. Her dad believed. Glancing at Tommy and Chris, she knew they believed as well. The excitement she was feeling was somewhat foreign, having not felt this way since her mother was alive. Those trips into the wilderness were special beyond compare, and this was the first time she'd felt this way since then.

Chris finished his story and they looked around at each other, excited by the possibilities. "We need to get your dad on board," said Jack. "Do you think you could do that?"

Shrugging, Chris answered without conviction.

"Maybe?"

"Head back to camp. Tell your dad about your experience and see if you can convince him we aren't making this up. Tommy, why don't you go with him, okay? And be careful! Stick together and stay safe. Sam and I will stay here to finish scanning the area. We'll join you back at camp once we're done."

CHAPTER SEVEN

S am and Jack continued their investigation, hopeful that Chris and Tommy would be able to get through to Charlie. "You think he's going to help?" Sam asked sarcastically.

"Who, Princess?" Jack was focused on his work, not paying much attention to anything else.

Sam, feeling like she was being ignored, sassed back. "Your *friend?* The one who wears a tin hat in search of aliens, but can't bring himself to believe this?"

"Sam, show some respect, please. He . . ."

"Respect? Like the respect he showed me? What, because I'm some little girl who doesn't know anything?" Sam was irritated at her dad's insistence that she should show respect merely because Charlie was older. Age was just a number. She took pride in her intelligence, even if she only chose to display it when it suited her needs. *Twelve going on twenty*, Jack would often remind her. She took it as a compliment. That feisty spirit was a gift from her mother and

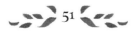

Jack appreciated that about her, even though he wasn't cut of the same cloth. He liked to think Sam acquired her quizzical nature from him, but that was probably from Nan too.

Jack continued, "I know. You're right. He just doesn't know you very well. He hasn't had a chance to see how smart you are."

Sam was livid at her father's defense of Charlie. "Why are you making excuses for him? He dismissed you, too. You saw, felt, and experienced everything I did, but he still chose not to believe. Even Tommy saw, but he didn't believe his own son."

Jack hung his head momentarily, realizing his daughter was too intelligent to try and appease with flawed logic. He raised his head to look at her and nodded. "You're right . . . you're always right. Just like your mom, too smart for your own good," Jack said humbly. "I'm sorry. I just hope Chris can get through to Charlie and convince him to put down his guard and trust us. Now that Chris had his own experience, maybe it will change Charlie's mind."

"I hope you're right, Dad, but I'm not holding out hope. I don't understand why he doesn't believe you, of all people."

"I think I know, Princess."

Jack recounted the story of Charlie's first breakthrough, although it had been more hypothetical than a proven theory. It wasn't that Charlie didn't believe or trust Jack—he most certainly did, and that's what frightened him. Charlie didn't believe in himself anymore.

Sam, curious as ever, had to ask. "Wait, Charlie

discovered something? Aliens?"

Jack put a finger up to his mouth to quiet Sam's sudden interest in Charlie, knowing she was mostly interested in what made him tick. She wanted inside his brain.

Years before, when Charlie and Jack were finishing up grad school in Washington, Charlie had volunteered as a teacher's assistant for a freshman-level astrobiology class. That particular course was the first step for would-be scientists wanting to explore the universe for signs of life. It had been one of Charlie's favorite undergrad courses. The class focused on the biology of life in space with little talk about intelligent life beyond Earth, but Charlie couldn't help daydreaming of extraterrestrials and the possibility that we aren't alone in the universe. *Are humans the most intelligent beings in the universe? If intelligent alien life exists, do they have the means to make it to Earth? If so, then we are undoubtedly the inferior species.* Charlie's musings would go much deeper, and it led him down a path that would become his life's work.

On the first day of class, Charlie took notice of a short-haired, golden-eyed coed sitting at the back of the lecture hall who bore a remarkable resemblance to a popstar he had been smitten with—Rihanna. He wondered if she had the same sultry and soulful voice, but he had never even spoken with her. Even though the room sat more than three hundred people, only twenty-three students were enrolled in the class. Ever the bumbling fool around women, Charlie was reluctant to strike up a conversation, fearful of rejection. His hesitation would go on for weeks. Luckily for Charlie, she eventually approached him, though purely for educational reasons. He was the TA, after all.

"Mr. Stevens? I have a question about this week's reading assignment."

Charlie tried his best to be calm, cool, and collected. "Please, call me Chuck." *Chuck? No one has ever called me Chuck. Why did I tell her Chuck?* It was too late now; he would forever be "Chuck." Between the class roster and having graded her papers, he knew full well who she was, but didn't want to be assuming. "And you are?" He felt like a schmuck.

"Diana. Diana Tanaka." She could see the confused look that crossed his face as his head tilted to the side, like a dog that heard a strange sound. Charlie was perplexed. He had scoured the class roster and was sure the girl standing before him was named Kristin. Before he could mutter anything, she interjected, "I'm adopted." She let out a small laugh. It was a big piece of information to share with a stranger, but she had grown used to it, having garnered those types of non-verbal responses throughout her life at the mention of her full name.

"Oh, uh . . . ok. I thought maybe you were married." Chuck looked away as he felt his face redden.

"Oh, heck no, not yet," she said, now blushing as well. "Chuck and Diana . . . sounds like royalty." She let out a snort and turned beet red as Charlie laughed hysterically. It put him at ease for the first time around her. Charlie and Diana got to know each other throughout the rest of that semester. She became his muse.

Jack had heard Charlie tell the story of their meeting too many times to count. As repayment for enduring the hours of storytelling, Jack would sometimes call him Chuck to throw a small jab, but always in good fun.

Jack attempted to continue his story, but was interrupted by Sam's very loud eye-rolling. "Come on, Dad, enough of the mushy love story stuff. What was Charlie's discovery?"

"I was getting there, Princess. So impatient."

It was Diana's question that day in class that led to Charlie's first theory; a question she was too embarrassed to ask in front of the other students, or to the professor, who was quite intimidating. Chuck was a friendly face, which made her feel safe. "What if we are the aliens? What if aliens are just humans from the future who have learned to time-travel, and we are the only form of intelligent life out there?"

Upon first hearing the question, Charlie's instinct was to dismiss such a far-fetched idea. But he was smitten, and wasn't about to show Diana his disbelief. "Go on," he encouraged.

"Well, think about it. Evolution." Charlie was unsure where she was going with this. "Throughout history, humans have evolved. Our heads have grown larger. Our eyes bigger and ears smaller. Our environment has transformed us from hunting, gathering Neanderthals to what we are now. Fire. Medicine. The Renaissance. The Industrial Revolution. The Internet and instant access to information. Every discovery has pushed humanity out of the cave and toward a higher level of intelligence. It's been exponential." Diana was spewing her hypothesis, barely taking a breath between thoughts. Charlie decided to give her a break.

"Okay, okay. Hold on. So what you're saying is that the advancement of human civilization is creating evolutionary changes in our appearance. And this makes us the aliens how?" Charlie was grasping for a conclusion.

"The way I see it, the enumerable growth of human intelligence is leading us to evolutionary and biological changes. Think about the typical representation of an extraterrestrial. Ask any fourth grader to draw you a picture, and what do you get? A skinny, pale figure with an unusually large head, big eyes and no ears. Is it really out of the realm of possibilities to think that could be a future version of us?"

The lightbulb in Charlie's head began to flicker. "Um . . . wow. I, uh . . ." He was speechless as he considered her proposal. He stared at her, not quite sure what to say.

Embarrassed, Diana turned away, not wanting Charlie to see the disappointment in her face. She had thought she could trust him with her hypothesis, as unlikely as it seemed on the surface. "I'm sorry, I have to go." She briskly started walking away, not wanting to face any criticism.

"Wait, where are you going? I want to know more! I'm intrigued, but I didn't know where to begin. I think you may have something here."

Diana swung around and wiped a tear from her eye as a giant smile formed. She re-approached Charlie. "Really? You don't think I'm crazy?"

"No, this is incredible. I want to keep talking about this. Would you want to work together, to put this on paper? Maybe hypothesize this for the larger astrobiology community?" Charlie fully embraced her ideas and wanted to push her theory forward.

Overjoyed, she ran up to him and hugged him, "Yes! Please, yes!"

Sam couldn't help but interject. "So Charlie thinks we are the aliens?"

"Simply put . . . yes," Jack confirmed.

"Okay, I'm confused. How did that discovery make him such a butthead? Wasn't the point of this story to explain why he doesn't believe us?"

"I wasn't finished. Are you ready to hear the rest?" Jack asked with a raised brow. Sam immediately fell silent.

Charlie and Diana worked on their hypothesis for more than a year. They perfected every detail. They answered every counterargument they expected to face. Once finished, Diana gave Charlie permission to use it for his grad thesis.

The day finally arrived for Charlie to present their work. In front of him, at a long, nondescript table sat three of his professors and his graduate advisor. As he began to deliver his hypothesis, Charlie was visibly nervous. Although his advisor generally knew what his work entailed, Charlie had never been comfortable with the reactions he received. Nevertheless, his advisor was curious and wanted to see where his studies had led him.

Chart after chart and argument after argument, Charlie

waded through his findings. He wouldn't wait for dismissive questions, but instead anticipated and answered them as part of his show to the panel. By the end, he was confident that his and Diana's work would be well-received, and perhaps garner a fellowship and grant to continue his research.

When he finished, the panel of scholars huddled in private to discuss what they had heard. Not one of them had asked a single question through the duration of Charlie's presentation. Some slight snickers started to make their way from the scrum, and Charlie could not help but feel they were mocking him. His advisor peeked his head up and glanced at Charlie, but did not give any indication before turning back to the discussion at hand. Charlie was growing more and more nervous, despite his confidence only moments before.

After five minutes, the head of the biology department, who chaired the board, turned around. The others followed suit, and Charlie noticed their solemn faces, even catching one of the professors shaking his head disapprovingly. "Son, I know you put a lot of hard work into this thesis, and I know that you believe what you've written and presented to us here today. However, it is the decision of this panel that this does not meet the burden of graduate-level work. You have provided us a fanciful theory without any proof. At this time, we cannot grant you any awards or honors. Thank you for your time."

Charlie's heart sank; tears welled in his eyes. Demoted, he turned and walked away, but not without hearing the laughter now coming from behind him. He had to go back to

Diana and deliver the heart-wrenching news. Unfortunately for both of them, that was just the beginning. Within a week, a story emerged in the school paper unveiling Charlie and Diana's theories. It was the talk of campus, but most of the chatter was full of laughter and ridicule. Although their names went unmentioned in the news article, everyone was keenly aware of the stars of this viral comedy. The editorial did not pull any punches, wrought with mockery and derision.

Charlie and Diana became the laughing stock of the school. They would endure what was now their legacy for the rest of the semester. Charlie and Diana never returned to school again, and the pain of that experience led to their eventual breakup. He lost all he had worked so hard for, and in the end, he blamed Diana and her theory for everything.

"Wow, Dad, that's awful," said Sam. "But, I still don't get it. You've almost always gone with Charlie on his alien trips, just like he comes on yours. He still believes, so why would he get so angry?"

"It's hard to say, Sam. Alien hunting is one thing, but to suggest that we are the aliens was perhaps too much for anyone to believe. The fact that we found something so foreign and unbelievable must have stirred up those old feelings for Charlie this morning. I'm not sure it mattered that I was the one trying to convince him." Jack kept the news of Charlie's divorce to himself; it wasn't his news to share, even if it would have provided some insight into Charlie's abrupt change of behavior.

"Well, I hope Chris can bring him around. It's all too amazing not to believe." Sam, despite feeling bad for Charlie, was as determined as ever to figure out what was going on in this forest. "I'll grab the scanner, Dad. Let's get back to work!"

Jack tossed her the scanner and smiled. "Right behind you, Princess."

CHAPTER EIGHT

Charlie sat quietly in his tent reading his notebook, calmer since the rush of earlier events. The bluish-gray, spiral-bound leather cover was well worn, as it contained his field notes dating back more than twenty years. As he flipped the pages, Charlie realized that perhaps he had been chasing ghosts. His life's work was contained neatly in one book, but he had nothing to show for it. No breakthroughs. No discoveries. No fame or fortune. His calm, even demeanor turned to sorrow at the realization that he had accomplished nearly nothing in all those years.

Despite the humiliation he faced early on, Charlie had managed to convince a small group of scientists at the SETI (Search for Extraterrestrial Intelligence) Institute to fund his work. However, he wasn't forthcoming about his theory. Instead, Charlie towed the astrobiology line, so to speak, as they believed he was researching rare minerals which might point to origins of life beyond Earth. In reality, he was still attempting to prove his beliefs about the future of

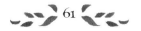

humankind. Unfortunately for Charlie, his grant was running out and his inability to show progress to those funding his scientific endeavors was growing tiresome. A few days before leaving for Arizona to meet up with Jack, Charlie was informed that barring some miraculous discovery, his funding would be cut in one month. It was salt in the wound with the loss he was suffering in his personal life.

Lost in thought, Charlie's focus was finally broken. "Dad, I'm hungry," whined Eli. "Can we make lunch?"

Charlie dragged himself from his tent, thoroughly depressed. "Sure. What do you want?" But before Eli could answer, Chris and Tommy came stumbling back into camp. "Back so soon?" Charlie asked.

Chris could tell his dad was not as hotheaded as before, which gave him pause. He wasn't sure he wanted to say anything that might cause things to revert. Chris knew he had to tell his father what he'd experienced in the woods, but was wary about the reaction he'd receive.

Tommy beat him to the punch, "We didn't really find anything." His white lie was simply to spare himself and his brothers from any further ire.

"Nothing really?" Charlie shook his head with a crooked smirk. "Is it something or nothing?"

"No, nothing." Tommy continued. Charlie knew information was being withheld—he knew his boys well.

Chris was more anxious than ever. He knew Tommy and Eli believed already, and now that he did, his dad wouldn't have a single skeptic on his side.

"What's going on, Chris? Spit it out." Charlie was growing agitated.

"They . . . they didn't find anything, but I did." Chris relayed his experience in exacting detail. With every sentence, he scanned Charlie's face for signs of disbelief or anger, but Charlie didn't offer a clue. He stood there, stone-faced, listening intently in complete silence. The lack of expression and questions was making Chris even more uneasy; he half-expected his dad to go nuclear at any moment. Chris finished his tale and nervously waited for a response.

Charlie leered at Chris with his arms crossed, taking in everything he'd just heard. He glanced over at Eli, who was clearly in awe of Chris' story but afraid to ask any questions himself. Charlie returned his gaze to Chris, and slowly a giant grin started to form. He tilted his head back and let out a guffaw, then reached out to Chris. Chris assumed he was about to be punished, but instead he was wrapped in his dad's arms. Charlie was jubilant. "Boy, you may have just saved your dad's bacon!"

Chris had no idea what Charlie was talking about. The father hadn't dared let on to the boys that they were about to fall on hard times. Eli, in his naivety and ever-present hunger, was already sidetracked by a package of graham crackers. All he knew was his dad wasn't mad, and that was good enough for him. Chris, however, needed to make sure. "You're not upset?"

"Upset? No! This is the lead I was hoping for. You experienced a real-life close encounter!" Charlie was ecstatic.

Chris started to smile but he was still nervous, having not yet revealed the complete truth about Sam, Jack, and Tommy's discovery in the cave. "Hurry up. Let's get some supplies together. I wanna check out the spot where this happened to you and see if there are any clues."

Eli only wanted to eat. He was having none of it. "But Dad, lunch . . . I'm starving."

"Grab an apple and some more crackers. I promise you we'll eat well tonight. Hopefully, there'll be reason to celebrate!" Charlie's over-excitement wasn't what Eli wanted to hear in that moment, but there was no convincing his dad otherwise. Charlie's exuberance was something the boys had learned to live with, as he would regularly drop everything at the most trivial minutiae that he thought could lead him to greatness among his peers. His thirst for fame, fortune, and redemption were unmatched.

Charlie grabbed his pack to start loading up supplies and immediately noticed something was missing. Chris, seeing this, was instantly aware of the wrath he was about to receive. Charlie looked up at Chris without saying a word. The look in his eyes requested an explanation.

In an attempt to save his hide, Chris fibbed. "I, uh . . . accidentally grabbed your stuff when I left last time. I didn't realize it until I got to the rock. Jack asked if he could use it. I figured maybe it wasn't a big deal since it would help prove them wrong." Chris didn't want his dad thinking that he was siding with Jack over him. He was anxious about the tension that had grown so quickly between the two old friends.

Charlie was so focused on Chris' strange encounter that the news of Jack having his thermal scanner didn't faze him. "No worries, I have a backup. Eli, get into the tool chest and grab it for me, please."

No worries? Chris was surprised by his dad's nonchalant attitude. It seemed the others were no longer a concern, which Chris found annoying given that Tommy was "on their side." He needed to make sure Eli was on board so that nothing would upset their dad the way the morning had.

"Here, Eli, let me help." Chris hoped his dad wouldn't notice the need to help his little brother retrieve a two-pound scanner from the toolbox in the bed of the truck. Charlie never looked up from what he was doing.

As Chris approached the truck, Eli asserted himself. "I got this, Chris."

"Shut up, butthead, and listen. You still can't let Dad know you believe the others. Just stay quiet about it, and hopefully, they'll find some more clues and be able to convince Dad that their Bigfoot findings are real."

"More clues? They found something?"

"Shhh. Yes, some burnt stones in the nest from the cave. But don't say anything. Let's just help Dad check out the other area."

"Wait, so did that stuff really happen to you? Or did you make it up to try and make Dad believe?" Eli was feeling a bit confused over what was real and fake.

"Yes, it did happen. But I think it has something to do

with what the others experienced. It may be something else . . . maybe alien. I don't know, but I'm not gonna tell that to Dad. Just go along with it for now, okay?" Eli nodded in understanding. "Good. Now let's go try and figure this all out."

Chris and Eli walked back toward their dad and Tommy and donned their packs. "Ready, Dad," Chris said.

Charlie took the scanner from Eli, placed it carefully in his sack, and closed it up. "Let's go, boys! Chris, lead the way," he demanded in giddy excitement.

As they made their way down the path, Eli could feel something moving against his back. Spooked, he stopped, dropped his pack off his shoulder, and quickly backed away. "Dad, there's something in my bag."

"What are you talking about, son?"

"It's probably moldy food come to life, to haunt you," Chris panned.

As they watched, something in the sack started to squirm. "Go ahead. Open it, Eli," commanded Charlie.

"No way! Chris, you open it."

"Not my pack, not my problem. That's all you, bro."

Eli quietly inched his way near, not wanting to rouse whatever was inside. He hoped it wasn't a snake—the one creature that frightened him more than anything. Charlie, watching as patiently as possible, was growing tired of the distraction.

"Move, I'll do it." Charlie reached out and quickly released the drawstring. As he did, the backpack fell over. A

nose poked out and sniffed the surroundings, but the scared creature promptly retreated.

"I think it's the ring-tail!" said an excited Eli. He reached into his pocket and pulled out another grape, offering it to the mischievous stowaway. Slowly, it emerged and gently took the food, this time eating it without running away. Eli placed out his hand for the cat to sniff; it started making clicking sounds and whipping its tail from side to side.

"Careful. I think that thing is getting ready to attack," said Tommy.

"No, it's not. It's just . . ." But Eli was caught off guard as the ring-tail pounced on his chest, causing him to fall on his back. Before he knew it, he was being licked to death by his attacker. Eli couldn't help but laugh.

"Are we done here?" asked Charlie. "We need to press on. Bring your little friend with you, but don't let it get in the way. Ok?" Eli nodded.

"What are you gonna name it?" Chris asked.

Charlie chimed in before Eli could answer. "How about Popcorn?" Chris and Charlie chuckled at Eli's expense. Tommy, still wary of his dad's hot and cold behavior remained quiet. Eli liked the name but wouldn't admit it, trying to hide his smile with a pout. Popcorn clicked his approval.

Soon, Chris stopped them at the edge of the path. It was a clearing roughly twenty feet wide and thirty feet long. Ponderosas lined both sides, but a window through the trees

allowed the now-waning afternoon sun to light the place where they stood. Chris placed a foot on the horizontal branch that had tripped him. "This was in the shadows earlier. I never saw it."

Charlie scanned the area, taking notice of the dirt ten feet beyond the branch showing where Chris had come skidding to a halt on his stomach. "Looks like you were safe," Charlie teased, referencing a baseball slide. Chris didn't find the joke funny.

Chris moved to the center of the clearing, where his "slide" had ended. He got down on the ground to reenact the scene for his dad and brothers, and explained how the sun was almost directly overhead at that point, but he was still covered in a shadow. He described feeling the heat on his back, and knowing it was certainly not the sun, as it was much hotter. He told them how the shadow had disappeared, and the sun reemerged.

Chris got up and dusted himself off. All of them looked up through the trees. The only opening that would have allowed the sun to light up the area where Chris had laid was directly overhead in the dead center of the clearing.

Charlie began his interrogation. "You're sure the sun was directly overhead?" Chris nodded. "How big was the shadow?" Charlie grabbed a small branch from the ground and handed it to Chris. "Draw it."

Chris took the branch and carved a groove in the earth surrounding where he had fallen, creating an eight-foot diameter area. Charlie moved to the center of the circle and

looked up, taking notice that the trees were roughly 150 feet tall. He pulled out his notebook and began to scribble furiously. Charlie was no mathematician, but he thought that by calculating the height of the trees and the position of the sun directly overhead, he might be able to estimate the size of the overhead object.

After a few moments of scratching on his notepad, Charlie stopped, looked up, and then looked back at his calculations. He was getting flustered at not being able to figure it out. He could have used Jack's help. Jack was excellent with numbers and always helped Charlie through difficult math challenges.

"Considering how much heat you say you felt, it's hard to imagine the craft was much more than a few feet higher than the treetops." Charlie, convinced that it was some sort of flying ship hovering, gave no thought to other possibilities. "It must have been quite large to throw that kind of shadow," he surmised.

Still looking for some tangible evidence, Charlie pulled the thermal scanner from his bag and turned it on. He began to scan the ground around the circumference of the shadowed area Chris had drawn. *Perhaps there are some residual heat signatures*, Charlie thought.

Nothing.

He looked up. *If only there was a way to scan the treetops. They're so close to the source, there must be a heat signature up there.* Charlie knew what he needed, but he likely wouldn't be able to get it . . . *Jack's drone!* If he could attach the scanner

to the drone, then he'd be able to scan the tree canopy.

As if his prayers were answered, Jack and Sam emerged through the trees. They had finished for the day and were headed back to camp, shocked to see Charlie and the boys standing there.

Jack warily spoke up. "What's going on, guys?" He kept Sam behind him, not sure what to expect.

Charlie ignored the fact that he had created such a scene earlier and immediately sought Jack's help. "Do you have your drone? We need to attach the thermal scanner and check the trees."

"What are you talking about, Charlie?"

"Didn't Chris tell you? About the alien craft?"

"Alien craft? I'm not sure what you're talking about right now, Charlie. And no, I don't have my drone. It's back at camp." The disappointment on Charlie's face was evident, but he remained even-keeled.

Charlie recounted Chris' experience, unknowing they had already heard it. Jack felt it was best to let Charlie believe they were clueless. As Charlie finished telling the story, Jack agreed to help him the next day. Despite a lack of remorse or an apology, he knew that helping Charlie might be the best way to get him to believe that something magical was going on in this forest.

"Can we go back to camp now? I'm starving." It was Sam grumbling this time.

Eli responded, "A woman after my own stomach." Popcorn poked his head out of the backpack and started

chattering, clearly hungry as well.

"Whoa, who's your friend, Eli?" asked Jack.

"This is Popcorn, the ring-tail cat. He's the one who snuck into my tent last night. Dad thought the name was fitting."

They all laughed as they turned their attention to the trail toward camp. The entire way back, the kids took turns holding and petting their new furry companion. It was a much-needed distraction from the long, exhausting day, and they were all famished.

CHAPTER NINE

The next morning, the group set out for another day of investigation. Charlie seemed to be in a better state of mind, and there was a calmness that wasn't present the previous day. The conversation was light, and the kids joked and poked fun at each other in their usual loving manner. Jack and Charlie discussed their days at university; Sam heard her dad call him Chuck and couldn't help but laugh. Tommy, walking shoulder to shoulder with Sam, laughed with her even though he didn't know why he was laughing. Charlie had never shared that story with his boys, not wanting them to feel sorry for him.

When they arrived at the first clearing, Charlie prepared for a long day of work. Jack, Sam, and Tommy never hesitated as they continued down the path, catching Charlie off guard. "Where are you going?"

"Back to the boulder. We set up more cameras before we left to see if we could catch anything," Jack replied. "I brought the laptop this time, so we can check the cards."

"You're still chasing butterflies, huh?" Charlie chided, shaking his head in disapproval. "Tommy said you guys came up empty yesterday. You're wasting your time, friend."

"I guess we'll see. I suppose if the cameras come up empty, then maybe you're right. But I saw enough with my own eyes to believe that something is going on there, no matter how illogical it may sound." Jack could feel the tension starting to rise and didn't want things to escalate, but couldn't help getting in a jab. "You'll know where to find us if you strike out here."

Charlie didn't respond as he unpacked the drone and fit it with the thermal scanner. He positioned it so he could use the drone's integrated camera at the same time and hopefully be able to pick up some indication of what happened the previous day. Chris and Eli stood by and watched their dad. They would have preferred to join the others, but could sense Charlie's frustration and knew they needed to keep up appearances.

Once the scanner was secured, Charlie powered everything on and the drone whirred to life. Controlling the craft would be a bit more challenging with the scanner attached, but Charlie had plenty of experience flying these things; he liked that it felt like he was flying a UFO. Eli loved to watch his dad in action and hoped that one day soon, he'd be able to learn the ropes and pilot a drone too. "Alright, here goes nothing," Charlie exclaimed. Chris shrugged his shoulders and nodded, unsure they would get any concrete results.

As Charlie took the drone up through the trees, he rotated the craft left and right, gaining his bearings while searching for anything unusual. Steadily, he climbed until he reached the treetops. A smug look crossed his face as the altimeter reading settled at precisely 150 feet. *Damn, I'm good*, he thought. Unfortunately, though, Charlie had let Jack go without getting any help figuring out his earlier calculations.

Now above the trees, Charlie panned the camera a full 360 degrees to get a view of his surroundings. The early morning sun, still rising, partially blinded the camera, but he could see the camp clearing to the east. Charlie brought the drone up to 200 feet and tilted it downward at a thirty-degree angle, allowing him to get a less obstructed view of the surroundings. He could track the trail for the most part, from camp to their current location. He continued to move along the path toward the boulder; however, the trees grew too tall and dense to follow much further. Taking the drone up to 400 feet and well above the treetops, Charlie could finally make out the group of Ponderosas encircling the area around the boulder. From their location, this was a nearly fifteen minute hike, but from up here, it seemed a small jump away.

Descending the drone back below the canopy top, Charlie began his examination. The thermal scanner showed nothing remarkable—as expected—given that it had been nearly twenty hours since the incident. Slowly, he moved the craft within inches of the treetops. Zooming in to get a close up of the foliage, Charlie noticed it. *It's charred!* He maneuvered the drone along the entire interior rim of the trees. *They're all charred!*

Chris could see his dad getting excited. "Dad, what is it? What do you see?"

"The trees are all burned. Every tree ringing this clearing shows signs of scorching. This is incredible!" Charlie continued to survey the trees. He handed the controls to Chris so he could make a note in his journal.

Eli looked up in jealousy, momentarily taking his attention from the PB&J on which he and Popcorn were snacking. "Should we tell Jack?" he mumbled with a mouthful of food.

"Of course! But first, we need to set up surveillance. If whatever caused this comes back, I want to catch it. Eli, how many cameras do we have?"

Eli stuck the rest of the sandwich in his mouth to free up both hands as he rifled through all the packs. "Uh, doesn't look like we brought any, Dad."

"No one thought to bring any cameras?"

Chris and Eli looked at each other and shrugged. "Sorry, Dad. I guess we weren't thinking," said Chris, as he carefully brought the drone to a safe landing.

"Hurry, let's go! We need to get back to camp and grab everything to set up a perimeter."

The others were just returning to the boulder. The chill in the air began to dissipate as they entered the clearing. Sam

quickly noticed that the leaves sat in perfect piles as she ran up to feel the boulder. "Ouch!" she proclaimed, clutching her hand as she jumped back. "It's really hot!"

Tommy followed suit, walking up to the rock as well. "Argh. Owww!" he exclaimed, shaking his hand to try and cool it off.

Sam shook her head, dumbfounded. "Really? Did you not just see me practically burn myself? Way to go, genius." Tommy felt two inches tall in that moment and was now more worried about what Sam thought of him than the pain pulsing through his hand.

"Ok, everybody, let's step back from the rock before anyone else gets hurt," Jack said. He untaped the thermal scanner he had attached to a large branch and staked into the ground about five feet from the rock. He waved the scanner inches from the surface of the boulder. *140 degrees.* "Stay here," he commanded. Jack swiftly moved to the cave side of the slab, being careful not to touch it. He could feel the immense heat emanating from the mouth of the cave; it was so hot that he couldn't get close enough to see inside. Wisps of smoke poured out of the opening and smelled like spices. *Nutmeg. Cinnamon. Is that frankincense and myrrh?* The smell instantly transported him back to his childhood; he oddly enjoyed the aromas of burning incense when his mother would take him to church on holidays. He held up the scanner to the entrance of the cave, barely standing the heat on his hand. *1200 degrees!!*

"Dad, what is it?" Sam shouted from the other side.

"Kids, get over here now! Do not touch the rock!" Sam

and Tommy scrambled over the berm to meet Jack. He tilted the LCD of the scanner so they could read it for themselves. "Call it a hunch, but I don't think we're dealing with a Bigfoot here."

"Then what? Wait, do you think Charlie could be right about the aliens?" Jack could only manage a quizzical shrug.

Jack flashed the light into the cave in an attempt to see inside. They could see that the dirt surrounding the cave entrance was blackened. Keeping their distance, they spied some larger branches, approximately six inches in diameter and fully intact.

"How are there still branches in there? Shouldn't it have completely burned at that temperature? It should all be ash." While no expert, Sam was smart enough to know that wood probably shouldn't have survived that type of heat.

"You're right, Princess. I'm not sure either. We need to check the cameras. Tommy, help Sam get the cards from the cameras. Try not to burn yourselves. I need to review the history on the scanner from last night." Jack sat down and flipped through screen after screen showing the temperatures in fifteen-minute intervals.

Midnight. *Nothing.*

1 AM. *Nothing.*

2 AM. *Nothing.*

Jack started flipping through the screens faster. Then he saw it, at 7:45 AM, just one hour before they had arrived at the site. The temperature spiked to 220 degrees on the heart-shaped divot. The temperature inside was surely hotter than

1200 degrees. "Sam, how's it coming with the SIM cards?" he yelled out.

"Tommy's getting the last one now."

"Get the laptop up and running, we have a time." Jack was excited but focused. He didn't want to get overzealous like his pal Charlie. He had learned early on that it often led to disappointment.

With the laptop powered up, Jack popped in the first card. He had set up three cameras: one aimed at the divot in the rock, one aimed at the pile of leaves, and one pointed at the cave entrance. He started the first playback from the camera pointed at the leaves. He slid the bar along the bottom of the screen, scrubbing to 7:40 AM, five minutes before the heat event. As the video resumed, they could see the leaves start rustling as a slight wind picked up. The wind should have been enough to send the piles scattering, but they remained intact.

Then, without warning, the screen turned bright white. It was as if someone had shined a flashlight directly into the camera, temporarily blinding it. Within seconds, the light flickered and then faded completely. The piles of leaves remained undisturbed.

Sam was the first to speak up. "What. Was. That?!"

Tommy shook his head in disbelief, his eyes wide and glued to the screen.

"I'm not sure. The other cameras should have caught it though. Give me the next card." Jack was a bit in shock himself, and growing concerned at what they might find on

the next video. It had barely been an hour since this happened, which meant that whatever caused this was surely still close by.

With the second SIM card installed, Jack fast-forwarded again to 7:40 AM. It was the divot footage. They all stared at the screen and waited for it. *FLASH!* As before, it faded in seconds, but what came into focus astonished them. The heart-shaped divot was glowing— shades of red and orange danced across the carving, fading into a brilliant blue before extinguishing seconds later. They looked up at the rock to make sure it was the same divot they saw on the video. Jack rewound the video to watch it again. They were all in disbelief.

"Dad, I'm scared," Sam admitted. Tommy grabbed Sam's hand, not to comfort her but to calm himself; frightened, but less vocal about his feelings. She allowed it.

"Me too, Princess. I guess we should check the last card." Jack steadied his palm to quell his fear. He was shaking as he ejected the card and inserted the final one, which would show the cave. Once again, Jack scrubbed to 7:40 AM. Before hitting play, he looked at Sam and Tommy. They all took a collective deep breath. "Are you ready?" They both nodded nervously, hands locked together tight. There were no thoughts of romance, only a desire to feel safe in that moment.

Jack pressed play. The minutes leading up to the event seemed to take forever, but not one of them took their eyes off the screen. Here it came. The winds picked up. The grass and leaves around the mouth of the cave started to move ever so slightly, then *FLASH!* The white light began to fade, but not entirely. The mouth of the cave returned to focus, glowing white-hot, impossible to distinguish anything inside, any movement behind the intensity of the light.

Jack removed his hat and wiped his brow, still focused on the screen. He let the video continue to play. The light faded slightly, just enough to allow for a sense that something was moving within the cave. The flickering and flashing of the light made it clear that whatever they were seeing was alive.

After another two minutes with only minimal movements visible, the light grew brighter and seemingly hotter. *FLASH!* When the image returned, the glowing cave was once again dark save for some embers within and sparks slowly floating out.

"Sir, can we please go back to camp now?" Tommy no longer cared if Sam saw how frightened he was. He wanted to leave immediately, and not chance running into something that might be unhappy to find them there.

Jack was singularly focused. He realized they had stopped the other videos well before the second flash. He grabbed the card with the footage of the leaves; it was zoomed out enough that the edge of the rock was visible in the frame. He went back and started the replay at the moment of the first flash and let the video continue. *Here it comes. Almost. NOW!* As the second flash faded, Jack saw it. He quickly looked at Sam, then back to the screen and hit pause. He didn't have to say anything.

"Is that . . . ?"

"I think it is, Princess."

"Is what?" Tommy chimed in, unsure what he was supposed to have seen.

Jack paused the video and pulled the bar back to the first moment the flash died down. There it was, clear as day . . . a tail feather. Bright orange and yellow, lined in reds, purples, and greens . . . and on fire. It was only in the frame for a second, but it was unmistakable.

"A phoenix," Sam answered solemnly and in partial disbelief at what they were seeing. Tommy could see it now. The still image sent chills through all three of them.

"It's not a myth," Jack said to himself under his breath. He turned to Sam and grabbed her, holding her tight, realizing they had stumbled upon something far more significant than anything ever seen before. "Princess, I think we did it." The fear they had been feeling faded as the magnitude of their discovery started to sink in.

Sam was enjoying the rare embrace from her father. She was equally ecstatic. "So much for Bigfoot," she panned, as she released herself from his grasp. She suddenly realized Tommy was still holding on tight to her hand and immediately pulled it back, not wanting him to think she was warming to his advances. At least not too much.

"Should we go tell Dad?" Tommy asked excitedly.

Jack quickly nipped his request. "Let's see if we can get a little more evidence before we tell him. I want to make sure this is concrete. We wouldn't want a repeat of yesterday . . .

Let's get these cameras reset in case it decides to come back."

They jumped to their feet to get the cameras ready. Jack positioned one of the lenses low to the ground, tilted toward the sky with one-third of the boulder visible in-frame, including the heart. The second and third cameras remained focused on the leaves and cave opening, respectively. Jack placed a special sun filter on the third lens, which would ensure the flash wouldn't blind the camera. He was confident that they would be able to capture the phoenix again, and provide substantial evidence to Charlie that something genuinely magical had happened.

Wow. Who would have thought? A phoenix. Is this real?

More than an hour had passed, and except for the thermal scanner, all the equipment had been reset. Jack decided to take one more reading of the heart and the cave. *600 degrees.* The chamber of the cave was cooling fast. He could now get close enough to see that the nest was fully intact. Despite the enormous temperatures, it hadn't entirely burned. *The phoenix's magic, no doubt.* He made his way around to the heart, where Sam joined him. *85 degrees.* He showed the scanner reading to Sam. She smiled, knowing what she had to do next.

Sam reached out and began to trace the heart with her finger. As expected, the winds picked up, and the columns of leaves began to dance and spiral into the air. Tommy, standing in the center of the clearing, began to laugh,

reaching toward the sky and spinning in concert with the leaves. They were in the presence of real magic. The myth of the phoenix was now a reality.

CHAPTER TEN

Charlie, Chris, and Eli gathered the cameras they needed to set up their UFO sting operation and made their way back to the clearing. Charlie was determined to catch evidence of alien beings or ships on film. He couldn't wait to share real evidence with Jack. This was supposed to be Jack's Bigfoot field trip, but he wasn't about to ignore evidence of the extraterrestrial variety. *I'll make it up to him. Maybe a Bigfoot trip to the Carolinas later this year.* He tried justifying the selfishness, and it was working. He wasn't about to let anyone stand in the way of the riches and recognition he'd receive once he had hard evidence of alien life.

Meanwhile, Jack, Sam, and Tommy had finished up and were making their way back. They had all sworn to stay mum about the phoenix. Tommy so badly wanted to tell his father, but knew Jack was right. Sam also threatened bodily injury, and Tommy didn't want any part of making her mad, nor his dad for that matter. He never wanted to see him that way again. It was a side of Charlie the boys had never seen.

As if by serendipity, both parties emerged through the woods and into the clearing at the same moment. Jack, Sam, and Tommy were smiling but had to contain any semblance of enthusiasm that might reveal their secret. Charlie and the boys seemed equally exuberant as they met in the center of the clearing.

"Empty-handed again, huh pal?" Charlie taunted. He looked at his watch, "A little early to be headed back to camp, no?"

Jack had his answer prepared and ready. "Not much for now. I reset the cameras and the thermal scanner. We'll check again tomorrow. I think we'll use the rest of today to head east and do some exploring." Sam, impressed by how her dad was handling Charlie, nudged Tommy with her elbow, a reminder to stick to the plan.

"That's too bad, Jack. Maybe you'll have better luck over there." Charlie started to pull the cameras from the backpacks. "I found all the luck I needed right here, thanks to Chris." He recounted what he found with the drone, showing Jack the images as proof of his discovery.

Jack feigned being impressed, knowing full well that an alien spacecraft wasn't responsible for Charlie's findings. "Wow, that's something! What can we do to help?" Jack wanted to keep Charlie focused on his wild goose chase and knew the best way was to join him.

Charlie's ego and greed kicked into high gear. "Not a thing, buddy. I think the boys and I can handle things from here. Just need to get the cameras ready to record." He wanted full credit for his discovery and had no desire to share the spotlight. Jack was already well known in his field, and Charlie didn't need him trespassing into his. "If you don't mind, I'll keep Tommy here; I could use his help." Sam glared at Tommy—one more reminder for him to stay quiet else he might get a visit from the tooth fairy. He sheepishly nodded.

"Sure thing," Jack replied. "Tommy, are you good with that?" Tommy nodded with a nervous smile. "Good. We'll see you later, back at camp. Happy hunting."

Charlie was glad Jack didn't push to help, but it also made him uneasy. Jack was persistent if nothing else, and would typically be adamant about sticking around to lend a hand. *Why did he give up so easily?* Charlie chalked it up to Jack's obsession with his own chase. He shook off his nerves and returned to the task at hand as Jack and Sam left to make their way back toward camp.

Once they were out of earshot, Sam expressed her concern. "Think Tommy can keep his mouth shut?"

"Have faith, Princess. I think Charlie is far too preoccupied with his own findings at the moment. Tommy will be fine. Let's get back and make lunch, then I want to check out the canyon rim. According to the map, it's about one mile east of camp."

"What about the phoenix? You don't think Charlie will find anything, do you?" Sam was concerned that Charlie would upend their discovery. She still didn't trust him, which only increased her apprehension about Tommy.

"That's why I want to check out the canyon. The phoenix has to be going somewhere when it's not in the cave. The canyon could be a perfect place for it to hide during the day. Too bad we can't get the internet up here. I want to know if there's any connection between the Native Americans in this area and the phoenix."

Sam's excitement grew a tad dim for a moment. "Too bad Mom isn't here. She'd know. She knew everything about the legend. She'd have all the answers."

Jack wiped a solitary tear from Sam's cheek. "She always did, Princess."

The walk to camp was silent, with Jack and Sam reflecting on Nan and what this moment would have meant to her. Her words now rang true more than ever. *It's only make-believe if you don't believe.* Sam played it over and over in her mind. Perhaps her mom sent the phoenix as a sign that she was watching over them, protecting them, healing their sorrow. Maybe she was giving them a reason to move forward and be happy again.

Back at the clearing, Charlie's video surveillance plan was coming together. They strapped one camera with a wide-field lens to a tree, angled up to catch anything that flew over the area. Two more cameras were positioned opposite each other to capture the clearing itself, with the trail in full view from both directions. It was the best they could do with the equipment they had. Ideally, Charlie would have placed the thermal scanner near the tops of the trees, but it would have been a near-impossible task. Instead, he staked the scanner in the dead center of the clearing, angled slightly to ensure any direct heat source from above would generate a relatively accurate reading.

"Are we almost done, Dad? I'm hungry," said You-Know-Who, Popcorn clicking in concurrence.

"Almost, Eli. Be patient. We need to get this right; there may not be a second chance." *This kid, his pet, and his appetite,* he thought. It was a wonder they had any provisions left, and it was only Day Three of the trip.

Eli reached in his sack to pull out a bunch of grapes and started snacking, giving every other one to Popcorn. The little cat's appetite rivaled Eli's in every way.

"Maybe we should've named that thing, Grape," Chris snidely offered. Eli ignored the dig.

Wanting to take one last survey of the area before departing, Charlie snatched the now scanner-less drone and brought it to life. Tommy wanted in on the fun. "Dad, can I fly it?"

Eli already green over Chris getting to fly it, didn't let Charlie answer. "No, there's no time for that! Besides, Dad won't let you." Charlie shot Eli a look to let him know he was out of line.

"Not this time, Tommy. Maybe tomorrow we can take it out for some fun, and we can all take turns." Eli lit up at the thought of finally getting his hands on the gadget.

Charlie proceeded with his ascent through the canopy. Once again, he took a slow approach around the inner rim of the trees, inspecting the leaves and looking for any additional clues from the burn pattern. Charlie didn't see anything unusual from this distance. He decided to take the craft up to 250 feet, where he could get a full view of the opening through the trees. Again nothing remarkable, as he couldn't make out the burn marks from this high. He proceeded up to 500 feet and panned 360 degrees, taking in the entire forest. He could see the canyon Jack and Sam would explore to the east, past camp.

As he slowly rotated toward the west, the exceptionally tall Ponderosas surrounding the boulder came into view. Charlie paused the aircraft and stared at the spot for a moment. *I could use another camera, and Jack doesn't need that many anyway. I don't think his wild goose chase will suffer if I borrow one.* Charlie's need to make history was clouding his judgment.

"We have one more thing we need to do." Charlie was speaking more to himself than to the boys.

"Dad, I'm starving," Eli moaned. Charlie put up a finger to silence his bleats without saying a word.

"What's left, Dad? We have this place covered pretty well." Chris was confused, not sure what else needed to be done.

"Not well enough. Get packed up; we need to head to the rock." Charlie quickly brought the drone to a safe landing and packed the remaining supplies.

A bad feeling started to well in Tommy's stomach, realizing what was happening. *What if Dad sees what we did? What if he sees the cave?* He attempted to stall. "Dad, I don't feel well. Can we just go back to camp?"

Charlie was having none of it. "You can head back if you want, but I need to borrow one of Jack's cameras." Charlie started moving toward the path with Chris and Eli trailing behind. Tommy just stood there.

"But, Dad?"

Charlie snapped around. "You know your choices here. Fall in line or fall back to camp!"

Chris jumped to Tommy's aid. "I'll take him back, Dad . . . is that ok?"

"Fine. Go!" Charlie turned and started down the trail, Eli nipping at his heels. They disappeared out of sight quickly.

"Let's go, butthead. You probably just need some lunch and you'll feel better." Chris turned and took a few steps toward the path before turning around to see that Tommy hadn't moved. He immediately sensed something was off by the look in his brother's eyes. "What's wrong? You look like you're gonna hurl."

"They can't go there, Chris. We need to stop them."

"What are you talking about? I know it's not cool for Dad to take Jack's camera, but do you want to be the one to tell him he's wrong? Besides, I'm sure Jack will be okay with it once Dad tells him why."

"We need to stop them. We need to keep them away from the rock."

"Okay, you need to spill it. What's this about?"

Tommy proceeded to tell Chris everything. The thermal readings. The glowing footage of the heart. The burned-out cave with a perfectly preserved nest. The phoenix. Chris stood in stunned silence by what he was hearing. Then the realization hit him as he looked up at the treetops—*the heat on my back, the shadow—it was a phoenix?*

"What should we do? I promised Jack and Sam I wouldn't say anything to Dad. I wasn't even supposed to tell you. Should we go tell Sam and Jack?"

Chris took a moment to think. "No, we need to stop Dad. If he sees the leaf piles or how the cave looks and feels, he's gonna know something's up."

"This is what I was trying to tell you all along!" They hastily grabbed their sacks and hurried down the trail to try and catch up to Charlie and Eli. They had some ground to make up if they were going to reach them before they got to the boulder.

Charlie and Eli were getting close. They could see the giant rock coming into view through the trees. Seeing it, Charlie laid out his instructions. "Let's make this quick. Get the camera, set it up, and get back to camp. Stay with me, Eli; this isn't the time to explore." Eli couldn't possibly think about exploring with his stomach growling. After all, it had been three full hours since his last meal, not counting all the snacks.

They stepped into the clearing, but panting and heavy breathing behind them in the forest caught their attention.

Chris and Tommy had finally caught up, and just in time.

"I thought you weren't feeling well?"

Chris answered for Tommy. "I gave him some water and an apple. He's feeling better."

Charlie looked Tommy up and down, shook his head, then turned back to scan the area for his plunder. His dad's nonverbal response made Tommy feel as though he'd let Charlie down somehow.

"Stay away from the rock, understand?" Charlie commanded. "We're not out here looking for Bigfoot. We have one job to do, and that's it."

Tommy took immediate notice that the leaf piles had fallen to the forest floor, and were scattered around the clearing. He wanted to feel the rock and see if it was still hot, but knew the trouble he'd find himself in if he disobeyed his dad now. Chris tried to push Charlie along and offered to help. "Will this camera here work, Dad?" pointing to the one aimed at the leaf piles. He could see the camera aimed at the entrance to the cave, and could tell there was a specialized attachment installed; it was clearly the most important.

"Pack it up," Charlie commanded. "Eli, get that one over there," he continued, pointing to the camera facing the heart.

Popcorn began to chatter loudly as if upset by the thievery taking place. "I thought we were only taking one," Eli cautiously noted.

"I changed my mind. We need them, Jack doesn't. And keep that rat quiet, will you?" Popcorn continued his ruckus

toward Charlie as he moved toward the thermal scanner and began to pull it off its wooden stake. Eli did his best to quiet the ring-tail, but it required another snack to make that finally happen. Even still, the hair on Popcorn's back was standing as he flicked his tail sharply.

With Charlie distracted and his back turned, Chris motioned to Tommy to grab the camera by the cave. Tommy shook his head, not wanting to disrupt Jack's operation, but Chris knew that getting that camera and keeping up appearances with their dad was more important. If Charlie were the one to retrieve that particular camera, he'd surely see the scarring on the ground and nest in the cave.

"Go!" Chris mouthed to Tommy in silence.

Tommy decided that maybe his brother knew best and swiftly rushed to the other side of the boulder. Once he reached the camera, he furiously began to unravel the tape that was binding it to the tree. He glanced back to see where his dad was, but Charlie remained hidden on the backside of the rock, still working on the scanner.

Tommy was seemingly taking forever. Chris moved to help him, but Charlie stopped him in his tracks. "What is this?!" Charlie screamed. Tommy feverishly continued to unwrap the camera on hearing the anger in his father's voice.

"What's what, Dad?" Chris asked.

"This! What are all these readings?" Charlie demanded as Tommy came back into view, having finished his job. "Tommy, you better explain what's going on and right now! What happened here?"

Tommy was scared. He hated lying to his dad, but he wasn't sure of the right thing to do. Luckily, Chris had his brother's back and jumped to his aid. "There was a fire." Charlie looked incredulously at Chris. "Tommy told me about it before we caught back up with you. Jack said the nest had caught fire and burned the cave entrance. He thinks the wind must've put it out."

Tommy wasn't sure where Chris was going with this. *You're telling him too much,* he thought. Charlie looked at Tommy, who responded before the question could be asked. "It's true. All of it." He tried saying as little as possible to avoid giving away his nervousness.

Charlie decided he needed to investigate the cave for himself. Tommy and Chris locked eyes, fearful as their dad made his way up the berm. As he did, he placed his hand on the rock to brace himself. Tommy had hoped it was cold and wouldn't burn him. *No reaction.* With Charlie almost out of sight, he reached out and felt that the rock was now cold. Colder than seemed possible, given the heat it had radiated just a short time before.

The boys scampered up behind Charlie as he attempted to peer into the cave. Charlie got down on his stomach to get a closer look. "Where's a flashlight? Somebody hand me a flashlight, now!"

The boys stared at each other, bewildered. "We don't have one, Dad. We didn't bring one," Chris replied. A wave of relief instantly came over Tommy, realizing his dad wouldn't get a clear view of the nest without the light. Charlie

jumped to his feet, still coursing over the cave entrance for answers.

"Well, there was definitely a fire here. But I have a hard time believing that the wind just knocked it out. It would've taken one heck of a gust to do that." Charlie noticed that Eli was still holding the camera he was instructed to take down and quickly realized that there should be something on film. "Give me that camera," he demanded. He inspected the camera and opened the slot for the SIM card. "Bingo," he exclaimed with a wicked grin. "Let's get back and set these cameras up. I want to know what's on this footage; my computer is back at camp."

Tommy and Chris no longer knew what to do or say. Tommy knew what his dad would find and he was afraid of the interrogation he would endure. If Charlie saw what was on those cards, he'd know everything. The boys felt helpless. In his anger at Jack for being less than forthcoming, Charlie never thought to ask Tommy what more he knew. Tommy only hoped it remained that way, for his own sake. Hopefully, Jack would be able to stop him once they returned.

CHAPTER ELEVEN

J ack and Sam made their way to the rim of the canyon wall, approximately one mile east of base camp. They stood at the white travertine cliff edge, overcome by the expansive views of the valley below. From their vantage point, they could see birds swoop in and out on rising streams of air, and small, dense patches of Ponderosas reaching for the top of the ravine, but falling short. A river carved its way through the limestone and several caves could be seen, one partially obscured by a low flowing waterfall cascading from fifty feet above.

Sam was mesmerized. "Any chance we can move camp here?" She yearned to wake up to this view for the rest of the trip.

"As wonderful as that would be, Princess, the trail's not wide enough to get the truck through and unfortunately, we have too much gear to hike in this far. I can't blame you, though. This is beautiful." Jack desperately wanted to give Sam what she wanted and scoured his brain for a way to make it happen, but couldn't manage a feasible solution.

Sam was disappointed, but knew her request was unlikely to be met with any real hope. "Can we at least hike down to that cave? Who knows, maybe Bigfoot is in there." Sam smirked at her dad in hopes she could pique his interest.

Jack laughed. "So the phoenix isn't enough for you, huh? What happened to 'So much for Bigfoot'?" Jack questioned with air-quotes, throwing Sam's words back at her in jest.

"Well, we shouldn't write off Bigfoot just yet, right? After all, that *is* why we came here." Sam was laying it on thick, attempting to get her way, but Jack could see right through her.

Jack looked down at the cave and saw that it would be a long hike down a series of switchbacks along the face of the cliff. "I tell you what, it's getting late and it's already been a pretty crazy couple of days, between Charlie's shenanigans and the phoenix. What do you say we head back to camp and relax for the rest of the evening? Tomorrow we can check the camera footage quickly, and if there's nothing new, we'll go to the cave. Sound like a plan?"

I suppose he's right, she thought. "Sure, Dad." Sam played sullen, dropping her head and looking up at him through her bangs, but her disappointment was just a ruse; she was doing cartwheels in her head. She actually wanted to get back to camp and get to bed, even though the sun would still be out for a few more hours.

Jack threw in a bonus for Sam being so understanding. "Maybe we can bring our sleeping bags and some supplies, and camp down there tomorrow night. Would you like that"

Sam's faux deception withered in a flash. She reached out to Jack with open arms and embraced him. Tilting her head up and donning her largest blue doe eyes, she pushed, "Can we sleep in the cave?"

"One thing at a time, Princess. Let's see what the morning holds, first." Sam bobbed her head in agreement. "Let's get back to camp. I bet Charlie and the boys are back by now. Maybe they'll want to join us tomorrow."

Sam's disappointment became apparent once again, this time for real. "Do they have to come? I'm sorry, Dad, but Charlie is just so . . . grrrr." Sam couldn't say what she wanted without being reprimanded for using adult language.

"I know he's not your favorite right now, but inviting them along is the nice and proper thing to do. Maybe now that he has his 'aliens' to keep him busy, he'll decline." Jack tried to calm her.

"I hope you're right. Besides, some quality father/daughter time without distractions would be nice. I'm just saying." She was back to her manipulative tactics, but Jack didn't mind. Time with Sam and no distractions sounded great to him.

Charlie and the boys made their way back to the clearing. He was still fuming at what could be on the cameras and Jack's insistence on hiding it from him. Tommy continued to stay

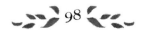

quiet and out of his dad's way, not wanting to get grilled about the footage and give up Jack's secret. Chris was doing everything in his power to help his brother in this endeavor.

Charlie checked his backpack for additional SIM cards to replace those in Jack's cameras and bring the footage from the boulder back to camp. *Only one card left. Damn!* Charlie proceeded to remove and pocket the SIM card from the cave-focused camera, assuming it would be all he'd need. *After all, that's where the fire was,* he thought.

Charlie set Jack's other two cameras to surveil the forest, positioned perpendicular to the trail, and placed the third camera containing the replacement SIM card facing skyward for additional coverage. Nothing was going to get through his optical net unnoticed.

"We're done here. Let's go."

"Thank goodness, I'm starving," said Eli.

Despite the gravity of the situation, Chris took the opportunity to bestow his littlest brother a new nickname, to provide some levity. "Let's go, Lunchbox. The faster we get back, the faster you can eat. Try and keep up." Chris began to sprint, leaving the others in his wake. Eli chased behind, Popcorn squeaking with every bounce of the backpack. Tommy wasn't laughing, but not wanting to be left behind alone with Charlie, he quickly caught up to Eli and pushed him aside to pass him.

Chris emerged into camp and immediately bent over to catch his breath. Moments later, Tommy and Eli caught up. "Not fair, Tommy pushed me, or I would've beaten you back,"

Eli moaned.

"Not a chance, Lunchbox." Chris was proud of the new moniker. Eli wasn't so sure.

"Knock it off. That's not my name." Popcorn put his two-cents in as well, clicking his disapproval at Chris. Eli quickly became sidetracked, rifling through bags of food in search of anything that would satisfy their hunger.

"Lunchbox, huh? Seems fitting," joked Sam as she and Jack reentered the camp. Eli glared at her, but didn't attempt a comeback with his cheeks already stuffed. "Where's your dad?" Sam asked curiously, not that she cared.

Tommy looked behind him, half-expecting Charlie to appear. They had left him behind to move at his own pace. He and Chris rushed to Jack and Sam. They only had a few minutes before their dad would be back. "Dad's coming," Chris began. "He took all of your cameras. He saw the cave and has the footage."

"Wait, you know?" Sam asked Chris.

Tommy confessed, "I had to tell him. I didn't want Dad to get the cameras, but we couldn't stop him."

Jack had so many questions, but they would have to wait. Before they could explain anything else, Charlie appeared at the trailhead. Upon seeing that Jack had returned as well, Charlie immediately got in his face. "So, you didn't find much? Trying to hide something, Jack? I saw the thermal readings. I saw the cave. What is going on?! I'm done with your games!" Charlie reached into his pocket and presented the SIM card, and Jack and Sam's eyes grew two sizes. Chris

and Tommy hadn't had a chance to tell Jack the story they told Charlie.

He didn't say he watched the footage, so he doesn't know about the phoenix yet, Jack thought. *That could be any card.* Jack decided to call his bluff. "Calm down, Charlie. There's not much to tell. Besides, you were on your own hunt, and I wasn't about to bog you down with details of my 'chasing butterflies,'" he offered sarcastically. "You made it abundantly clear that you weren't interested in our work at the rock. But since you've selfishly destroyed our investigation in search of your UFO, go right ahead. Watch the film yourself. See what we saw, and maybe you'll stop acting like such a goon."

Charlie stomped over to his tent and retrieved his laptop. No one said a word while it booted up. Jack, Sam, Tommy, and Chris exchanged stares, worried that their secret would get out. Jack could see the jealousy in Charlie's eyes and knew that keeping the discovery of the phoenix hush was paramount. In that moment, they were at the mercy of Charlie's greed.

He pushed the card into the slot on the laptop, waited for the video to load, and hit play. The group stood there, gripped by trepidation over what Charlie was about to see. Eli, not privy to the secret, positioned himself over his dad's shoulder to catch a glimpse of the screen. Popcorn laid in his arms, also seemingly interested.

Charlie stared intently at the footage, waiting, but nothing was there. The cave was in frame, but aside from leaves slowly blowing across the opening and some movements of grass, the film was a bore. "What is this? What am I supposed to be seeing? There's nothing here. Where's the other SIM card?" Charlie demanded, assuming Jack was hiding the footage on a different card.

Jack made his way over to see what was on the screen. "There is no other card. Whatever is on that card is what I captured. A whole lot of nothing." For the first time, Jack could see that it was the cave video. The phoenix never showed itself from this view, except for some mostly imperceptible movements after the first flash. He was somewhat relieved, but then noticed the scrub bar at the bottom of the video. The first flash was coming up in about twenty seconds, and that would open up questions he wasn't ready to answer.

Not budging from his stare, Jack knew he had to take a drastic measure. He grabbed the laptop from Charlie's hands. "Let me see this thing," Jack exclaimed. Just as the screen turned from Charlie's view, the flash occurred. *He didn't see it.*

The exchange riled up Popcorn, who jumped from Eli's arms onto the laptop, the creatures little paws hitting the scrub bar and fast-forwarding the video by a few minutes. Charlie snatched the computer back, unaware that several minutes of footage had gone unseen. "Eli, control that monster, now! Jack, I'm watching every last second of this thing whether you like it or not." Jack relented, knowing Charlie would surely see the second flash. Charlie continued

to watch with Jack now looking over his shoulder. Charlie turned and scolded, "Do you mind?"

Jack stepped back, dejected. Any moment, Charlie would see *FLASH*. "What the . . . ?" *He saw it*. Charlie continued to stare at the screen, watching for any more activity. The cave smoldered but nothing else occurred. "What was that?"

Jack hoped the answer that popped into his head would suffice. "Dry lightning."

"You can't be serious, Jack. You think that was lightning?" Charlie asked incredulously.

"What else could it be?" Jack would play dumb as long as possible.

Charlie shook his head and laughed. "You think that based on what Chris experienced at the clearing, and now this, that this is lightning? Wow, Jack. You're pressing there. How could this not be evidence of UFO activity?" More than ever, Charlie was convinced that the rock and his findings at the clearing were interconnected, and extraterrestrial life was the only reasonable answer. "First thing tomorrow morning I'm gonna go check those cameras, and I can't wait to prove you wrong."

Sam's disgust of Charlie was now unchecked. "Well it's too bad you stole all our cameras, because now you're not going to see a thing!"

"Oh darling, you're quite right, I did take them. But two of those cameras have additional footage if I'm not mistaken, and as I recall, one was aimed slightly up. So I'm going to take a stab and say that there's something else there. Come first light, I'll be retrieving the other SIM cards and I'll get to the bottom of this." He turned to Jack. "What's wrong, buddy? Afraid I was gonna find out your secret? I spend my life searching for alien life and you want to horde all the evidence and keep it for yourself. This is MY discovery! I would've shared the glory with you, friend, but you've just shown me who you truly are. You're a liar and a coward."

Jack said nothing. He looked down, grabbed his backpack and threw it over his shoulder, then made a beeline for the trail, going to retrieve the other cards. Before he could make his way across camp, he heard a familiar sound—the chamber of a shotgun being cocked and loaded.

"Oh, you're not going anywhere. That is my footage, and my new best friend here agrees," Charlie threatened, referencing his gun.

Jack stopped in his tracks.

"I know you have something on those SIM cards you don't want me to see or know about. There is something you aren't telling me, and I'll be damned if you are going to take this discovery out from under my nose."

They could all see that Charlie was a bit unhinged, and it wouldn't do any good to argue with him. The kids looked downright terrified, so Jack decided to let it be until Charlie had a chance to calm down. Not another word was spoken for the rest of the night. Jack and Sam retired to their tents, unable to talk or formulate a plan. Charlie kept watch over the entire group, careful not to let anyone out of his sight.

After several hours, the fire died out and snoring echoed throughout the camp. Charlie slipped into his tent to get some rest with the gun by his side. Sam's eyes opened, wide awake at the sound of Charlie's tent zipping up. She laid there silently on her back, staring at the roof of her tent. She knew what she had to do. She waited.

CHAPTER TWELVE

S am could feel the blood pulsing through her veins and her heart racing as she waited for the right moment to put her plan into action. She pressed the home button on her phone. *3:13 AM.* She would wait until the bottom of the hour to be sure, but she didn't sense any movement in the camp, especially from Charlie's tent.

Prepping to make her move, Sam grabbed her flashlight. Because it was too bright, she would have to wait to use it until she was out of view. For now, she'd use her phone and pray her battery would hold out. *15% battery. I hope it'll last.*

At 3:30 AM, it was time. Sam dimmed the flashlight on her phone to the lowest setting; just enough to stealth her way to the path. One inch at a time, she gently opened her tent, unzipping only far enough to squeeze through. As she stood up outside, she took a moment to look around. Everything was dark and quiet except for some snoring, including from Charlie's tent. Just what she had hoped. However, Charlie's

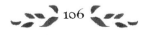

tent was the closest to the trailhead, and sneaking by wasn't going to be easy.

Sam decided to take the path heading toward the canyon. She'd cut through the forest and double-back through the trees until she was moving toward the clearing. Her plan was underway. She would get the SIM cards and slide back into camp before anyone knew she was gone.

Finally far enough out of camp, Sam shut off the flashlight on her phone, but not before checking the time and battery level. *3:45 AM. 3% battery!!* The light drained the battery more than she'd anticipated. She had less than two hours before dawn would break and everyone would rouse. She slipped the phone into her pocket and flipped on the proper flashlight with her other hand. Her surroundings lit up. *Better.* She knew she was taking a big chance going off course, but it was the only way to stay unseen and unheard. It didn't help that it was a moonless night, so keeping her bearings would be even more difficult.

Sam decided to keep track of her steps. *Turn left off the trail. Three hundred steps directly through the trees. Turn left again. Then I should be headed back toward the clearing.* She started to make her way through the trees. Despite being in the middle of a pitch-black forest with any number of nocturnal creatures watching her every move, Sam's focus was on one thing only.

Two ninety-eight, two ninety-nine, three hundred. Sam turned left and started back toward the clearing, stopping on occasion to survey the area to her left, making sure she wasn't getting too close to camp.

After about a half-mile, she heard a faint sound; a crack, followed by a warm rush of air through the trees. She stopped dead in her tracks and immediately turned off the flashlight. *What was that? Branches? Lightning?* She turned a full circle, taking in everything she could, but her eyes were struggling to adjust to the dark. She couldn't see a thing and was unable to locate the direction from where the sound emanated.

Sam was sure she was well clear of camp and should be meeting back up with the trail soon. Confident that whatever she had heard was an aberration, she continued. She made her way another two hundred yards through the trees, and was starting to get scared. She couldn't see the trail. *Did I make a wrong turn?* The moment of confusion was fleeting, as a flash of light lit up the sky above, accompanied by a deafening crack. Sam looked up, and behind the backlit clouds, a dragon-like shadow came into form. *The phoenix!* It appeared to be circling. Its bright flames engulfed the forest around Sam in dancing shadows. Her necked craned, Sam stared in awe, but her concentration was quickly broken by the hollering coming from the direction of base camp. *They saw! They know I'm gone!* She could hear the faint sound of her name through the trees. *Dad.*

With the forest still bright, Sam was able to see far enough through to realize she had made it back to the trail. She was only fifty feet from it the entire time. Correcting her course, she started running toward the clearing, knowing she was less than a minute away. Sam had to get there before

Charlie; he was surely on his way.

As she made her way into the clearing, the light from the phoenix faded and disappeared. Sam flicked her flashlight back on and swiftly made her way from camera to camera, cutting each down with a knife she had pilfered for protection. She didn't have time to open them and grab the cards; she would have to snatch them and keep running. *Charlie can't catch me, or I'll be dead.*

With all six cameras stuffed into her backpack, Sam kept moving. The sounds of Charlie and the rest of the group were getting louder; it was only a matter of time before they would break into the clearing. She could hear her dad even clearer, calling her name over and over. *The rock,* she thought. Sam jumped back on the path and made her way toward the boulder.

Five minutes later, the crisp night air echoed with the unmistakable sound of anger and disappointment. "No, no, no!!" It was Charlie. Sam grinned, knowing she had succeeded . . . for now. "I'm going to find you, little girl. You have no idea who you're messing with." The threat reached her, clear as a bell.

Get to the rock. Sam was scared, but focused. She ran as fast as she could, the weight of the backpack slowing her down ever so slightly. *I need to get there.* She wouldn't stop, refusing to look back. Her mission wasn't complete until the evidence was gone. Sam continued to run, nearly out of breath. *I don't remember it taking this long to get there.* In her fright, the trail appeared longer, and the boulder farther away.

Just as she had that thought, it appeared through the trees. Instantly, she could see the heart glowing bright, leading her to the finish line. The leaves were still in their piles. She wanted to touch the heart, but it was white-hot. The heat emanating from the rock was abundant and removed the chill from the air. Sam threw the pack to the ground with no care for the fragility of its contents. As she knelt to release the drawstring, a flicker of light caught her attention. Sam stopped what she was doing and looked up. It was coming from the backside of the rock. *The cave.*

Apprehensively, Sam made her way up the berm. The heat hit her face, and the light grew brighter as the mouth of the cave came into view. She couldn't believe what she was seeing. Feathers. Fire. *The phoenix!* It filled the entire space of the cave. It was enormous. She should have been scared, but she was instinctually at peace. Perhaps the stories her mother had told put her at ease, knowing that a phoenix would not bring harm to a human. It was beautiful. Its long, graceful neck glowed a soft blue, lined in oranges and yellows. Its body and feathers were radiating the same hues, different from what they had seen on the camera. Then Sam heard it for the first time—a low, subtle cooing sound accompanied by an odd chirp, unlike any bird she'd encountered. The phoenix was calm and content. It knew Sam was there, and that she wasn't a threat.

"Hi there," Sam said, attempting to communicate. Its giant green eyes scanned the girl, the cooing and chirping now a bit louder, as if to return her greeting. But the meeting

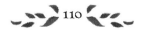

was short-lived. Without warning, the bird suddenly got agitated. It started flapping and fluttering its wings inside the cramped cave. Sam backed up, afraid of what might happen. She could see the colors of the phoenix changing with its mood. Dark reds and purples replaced the blues and oranges. The brightness engulfing, Sam was forced to avert her eyes. The firebird let out a screech and flew out of the cave, coming within inches of Sam's head. As she watched the phoenix take flight, she felt her hair, worried it was on fire. *Hot, but not burned.*

As the bird disappeared above the clouds, Sam could hear the incoming voices. It had sensed the group coming and was warning her, or perhaps it was just escaping from danger. Either way, Sam realized that she still hadn't taken care of the cameras. She jumped to her feet and slid down the berm, grabbing the pack just in time. Charlie, Jack, and the boys had just arrived.

"Put that backpack down now!" Charlie demanded.

Running on adrenaline and instinct, Sam scurried back up the berm to escape. She hadn't seen that Charlie was holding the gun, but as she reached the peak of the hill . . . *BOOM*, a blast rang out. She turned in horror to face the group. Charlie was reloading.

Jack feared for Sam. "Princess, please, listen to what he says. It'll be ok."

Out of the corner of her eye, Sam could see that the nest was smoldering. Chris noticed her glance and could tell what she was thinking. "Why should I listen to him? He's trying to

take everything from us. He's a bully!" Sam wasn't sure where this courage was coming from, but in spite of the gun, she wasn't ready to back down.

"Girl, I suggest you listen to your daddy, so you don't get hurt," Charlie bargained, the gun pointed to the sky. "Why don't you start by telling me what you just saw? We all saw the lights. We heard the sounds. You have two choices: tell us what you know or hand over the cameras. Either way, I'm going to find out what's going on."

Sam weighed her options. She wasn't going to tell Charlie anything, which left the cameras as the only proof. She took a step toward the cave and lifted the backpack over the opening, ready to drop it. The heat in the cave would surely melt the evidence quickly. "Back off, or I destroy the cameras."

Her bluff was useless against Charlie's weapon. "How about you back off and no one gets hurt." He lowered the gun and aimed at Jack. Sam no longer had a plan. The thought of losing her dad was too much to bear. She dropped her guard and slowly lowered her arm in defeat, moving the pack to her side. "That's what I thought. Now, bring it over here."

Sam took one step away from the cave, then *FLASH, FLASH, FLASH.* Sam had closed her eyes just in time. *FLASH, FLASH, FLASH,* again. Charlie and the boys were stunned and rubbed their eyes, not able to see. Jack was having trouble as well, but took the opportunity to shove Charlie away and run for Sam.

As Jack reached his daughter at the top of the hill,

Charlie got back to his feet and swung the gun around toward them. From seemingly nowhere, Popcorn jumped toward Charlie, biting him on the hand. *BOOM.* The deafening sound of the gun going off startled everyone. Jack and Sam checked themselves, but thanks to Popcorn's heroics, the shot missed.

FLASH, FLASH, FLASH. Sam now realized that it was the phoenix protecting them! Saving them. Jack grabbed the backpack and threw it into the cave. It immediately caught fire. "Let's go!" he said to Sam. She grabbed his hand and they ran into the forest, well off the path. Behind them, they could hear and feel the wind picking up. Sam glanced over her shoulder and could see a torrent of leaves engulfing the boulder just as one more parting shot from the bird aided their escape. *FLASH, FLASH, FLASH.*

Jack and Sam didn't stop. They ran through the gauntlet of trees for what seemed like a mile—sliding down hills and jumping over creeks, changing directions to try and lose Charlie and get to safety. Finally, they slowed down, sure they were out of harm's way, for now; but before they could catch their breath, something came charging through the woods hot on their tails. *He's got us,* Jack thought. As they turned around to meet their fate, Chris, Tommy, and Eli appeared. "Wait for us," Chris panted.

"Where's Charlie? What happened?" Sam asked, fear still gripping her.

"Still back at the rock. Tommy touched the heart, and when the wind picked up, a branch broke off one of the trees and knocked Dad to the ground. So we ran. I've never seen him act like this. We don't feel safe around him anymore. Can we stay with you?" Chris requested.

"By all means," Jack replied. "You boys are safe here. I think we need to stick together until we can figure this out."

"I saw the leaves as we were running away. That was you, Tommy?" Sam asked. Tommy nodded in silence, still in shock from everything that just happened. "Your fingers. You must've burned them." She grabbed Tommy's wrists and turned his hands up. Nothing. Not even a scratch, let alone any burning or charring. Sam gave Tommy a big hug, thankful for his bravery, then turned to her dad. "It was the phoenix. It saved us. The flashes. Tommy not getting burned. The branch. It helped us escape. Dad, I saw it. It let me get close." She continued to tell her dad and the boys of the moments before they had arrived at the rock. They listened in amazement, stunned by the reality of the phoenix and how it had saved them.

"We need to keep moving. Charlie is surely looking for us by now." Jack led the group through the thicket of trees and bushes, making their own path as they pushed forward. They hoped to find a trail soon and shelter to rest, but for now, they knew they had to keep moving to stay safe. The sun was rising. Soon they would have to determine where they were and what to do next. They were exhausted, and the day was just beginning.

CHAPTER THIRTEEN

The group had been walking for the better part of an hour. Still unsure which direction to take, Mother Nature took over and made the decision for them. They had come to a small canyon, forcing them to move south, along its rim. To head north meant they'd need to find a way up and over a series of large boulders stacked over a hundred feet high that bordered the canyon; to go around would require heading back toward the rock, and Charlie. The view from here was spectacular, but they were too tired, too hungry, and too distraught to take notice of the beauty surrounding them.

"Can we stop and rest? My feet hurt," whined Eli. Popcorn popped his head up, rubbing his front paws together, feigning exhaustion despite being carried the entire time.

"Sure thing, Eli. I think we've been moving long enough. It's time we come up with a plan, and the first thing we need to find is water." In their haste to chase down Sam and the mysterious light earlier that morning, no one had thought to bring any water or food. Sam, too, was ill-prepared, not having imagined that her middle-of-the-night special ops excursion would result in a wilderness survival challenge.

Everyone except Sam took a seat. She was weary, but didn't see fit to rest until they had water, food, and shelter. "I'm going to scout up ahead," she said.

"Are you sure you don't want to rest for a few minutes, Sam? We don't know how much farther we'll have to go yet. We should regain some energy." Jack was worried that Sam would push herself too far, but knew she was too bullheaded to listen. It was a futile attempt, but he had to try. Sam started to walk away. "At least take someone with you, please." Jack looked around the group.

Chris began to stand, but before he could get to his feet, Tommy sprang up. "I'll go with her," he said, looking sternly at Chris to sit back down.

"Ok, good. Be careful, please. And be back here in thirty minutes," Jack instructed. He threw Tommy his watch, but not before setting the timer and starting the countdown.

"Yes, sir." Tommy caught the watch and strapped it to his belt loop.

"Let's go." Sam wasn't happy about having to be chaperoned, but if it was going to be anybody, she was glad it was Tommy. He was growing on her. They had been through so much in just a few days, and she was indebted to him for helping them escape.

As they made their way through the trees and out of

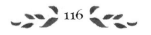

view of the others, Sam finally let her guard down, looking back at Tommy and flashing him a crooked smile. "What?" Tommy inquired, lagging. He sped up to walk by her side.

"Nothing. I'm just happy you came along. You were very brave to do what you did."

Tommy blushed, not sure what to say. He was smitten with Sam, had been from the beginning, and she seemed to be warming to him. "Thanks," he meagerly replied.

After several more steps in shy silence while trying to make sense of their feelings, Sam stopped suddenly and motioned to Tommy. "Do you hear that?"

"Hear what?"

"Shhh," Sam demanded, pointing to her left toward the interior of the forest.

Tommy's eyes slowly widened as he identified the sound of bubbling, swishing, and sloshing. It was unmistakable. "Water."

They wasted no time running toward the source, Sam leading the way. As they got closer, the rushing water grew louder until they finally came to the bank of a broad, rapidly flowing creek, covered by a massive grove of shade trees.

"Yeah!" Tommy shouted with joy. Sam laughed in delight. They both knelt and started scooping water into their mouths. It was cold, and tasted like something you'd buy in a fancy bottle. They couldn't get enough, but thoughts of the others quickly set in. "We need to go tell everyone," said Tommy.

Sam looked up from her makeshift trough. "Definitely,

but first one more drink." As she bent to take another sip, a bright light broke through the trees and reflected off the water, nearly blinding her. Sam moved her head, and the reflection seemed to follow her. She held out her hand to block the light while looking for the source—the angle was too low to be the sun. It forced her gaze downstream, revealing an opening through the trees. "Tommy, look!" She pointed down the bank of the creek.

Sam quickly started making her way downstream, with Tommy tagging along. Just one hundred yards from where they had just imbibed, the stream of water disappeared. As they got closer, they could see the end. The water, plummeting over the canyon wall in a spectacular display, sprayed a rainbow of mist which hung suspended over the ledge. Had they continued along the cliff edge from the beginning, they would have found this spot regardless.

They stood in awe for a few minutes before Tommy broke the silence. "Wow, now we really need to go get everyone." Sam nodded her head in agreement, not wanting to budge from her spot. She grudgingly walked backward before finally breaking away to join Tommy.

As they turned around, a sudden, warm rush of air blasted them from the canyon below. Sam turned just in time to see the phoenix soar through the mist of the waterfall and high into the blue sky. *The light, it was the phoenix!* Sam thought. The bird made a giant loop before swooping past them at full speed. After circling back, it joined the kids at the side of the cliff, chirping and cooing while hovering above the

crevasse. It was attempting to tell them something, but neither Sam nor Tommy could understand the creature.

Sam noticed the bird's colors. Its red head with large emerald eyes faded into oranges and yellows, lined in blue fire. On top of its head sat a blue crest of flames that maned the bird's back down to the tail feathers. Deep red feathers covered its neck and chest, then changed into oranges and yellow in its tail, matching the enormous wings. They were the same bright hues as when she had first come face to face with it, not the deep, dark colors it flashed when it became agitated. Sam took it as a sign that the phoenix was calm and in good spirits.

Slowly, the phoenix flapped its wings, wisps of fire jumping from their tips with every movement. It glided forward and came to rest on top of a large rock. The chirping and cooing continued as it stretched its long neck and motioned toward Sam, flicking its head up and down. Sam was mesmerized by the dancing, colorful flames, and moved toward the giant bird without a second thought.

"Sam, be careful," Tommy said, barely above a whisper. With Tommy's plea came a new sound from the bird; a short, reverberating whistle now accompanied the previous sounds. Sam continued, unafraid.

"Should we try this again?" she asked the phoenix. The bird cooed in approval, or what Sam took as approval. "I don't suppose you have a name? Or at least one I can understand?" The phoenix chirped, but the language barrier was apparent. Sam knew she could tell its moods by its colors, but trying to make sense of its sounds was nearly impossible. "I'm not sure what you're saying, but how about I call you Ash? Does that sound okay?" She remembered from the myth how these birds rise from their ashes, being reborn every thousand years. The name seemed fitting. The phoenix joyfully chirped, cooed, and whistled. "I'll take that as a yes," Sam replied, laughing.

Tommy stood there, awestruck by what he was watching, but was snapped back by the sound of the watch's alarm beeping. "Sam?" He waited for an answer, but she was fixated on the bird. "Sam, we need to go and get the others." Again, no response. "Sam!" he yelled. Ash flapped its wings and let out a screech. Tommy jumped back. The bird's feathers flashed dark red before returning to their soft colors and retucking its wings.

"Tommy, stop! You're upsetting him. When he changes colors, it means he's getting mad," Sam scolded.

How could she know that? But he didn't dare question her out loud. "Sorry. But we really have to get back to the others, and let them know about the water."

"Fine," she relented, turning back to Ash. "We need to go. We haven't had anything to eat or drink in hours." She was unsure the bird understood what she was saying. Ash cooed and moved his head down to Sam's level, like a dog looking for a pat on the head. She reached out tentatively and placed her hand on his head. *It doesn't burn.* The warmth from the phoenix made its way through her hand and up her arm. Startled by the sensation, she pulled her hand back, noticing the bright orange imprint of her hand on his head, which slowly dissolved back into red. "We'll be back soon, okay?" Ash whistled in concurrence.

Sam backed away and turned toward Tommy, solemnly walking past him without a word. He glanced down at Jack's watch. They had already been gone for over thirty minutes and still had to hike back. "I'm sorry, Sam. I want to stay longer too, but we're already late getting back, and we need to tell them about the creek . . . and Ash."

"Then let's hurry. Race you back?" Her mood instantly lightened as she couldn't wait to share the news with her dad. She took off like a flash, leaving Tommy in the dust. The whole way back, Sam was screeching and cooing, chirping and whistling—doing her best to imitate Ash.

She raced back to the rest spot, but when she got there, everyone was gone. "Guys? Dad?" she yelled out. *Where did they go?*

Tommy pulled up twenty seconds later. "Where is everyone?".

"I don't know, but I have a bad feeling about this, Tommy. They wouldn't just leave us. They knew what direction we took."

"My Dad must have caught up. It's the only thing that makes sense. What do we do, Sam?" Tommy said, scared.

"Ash. Maybe Ash can help us find them," she posed. "We need to get back to the waterfall." Tommy nodded, and they immediately turned tail and headed back, hoping Ash would still be there.

Jack marched forward, retracing the same path they had created in escape, now flanked by Chris and Eli. They moved sluggishly back toward the rock, unsure what fate awaited them. Jack's wrists were bound with a strip of Chris' shirt; makeshift cuffs, courtesy of Charlie. Gun at the ready, Charlie stayed close behind, keeping a watchful eye for any signs of mutiny. Despite the boys' rebellion, he didn't feel it necessary to restrain them, but ensured the "rat" wouldn't provide any further heroics by cinching Popcorn tight into Eli's backpack.

"I'm disappointed in you boys. I can't believe you'd help them get away and hide something like this from me. We're supposed to be a team." Charlie talked to hear himself speak, to break the silence on the long walk. His calm tone made the situation feel more horrifying than it already was. "I was wrong. I'll admit that. I didn't believe in whatever it was you were chasing. Who would have thought . . . a real live phoenix? I suppose some myths are real. Here I was tracking aliens, and you were the one with something real all along. Just not sure where we went wrong, buddy. We could have figured this all out together. But I guess that doesn't matter anymore. You betrayed our friendship, so kiss your discovery goodbye. I'm going to get my hands on that thing and show the world."

Charlie's delusions of grandeur were controlling his every move. Jack wasn't sure what he could do to stop him. His thoughts immediately turned to Sam. By now, she would

have realized that they were gone and hoped she wouldn't run to help them. *Maybe there's a park ranger she can flag for help.*

"Dad?" Eli hesitantly spoke up.

"Son, I don't want to hear from you right now. I know . . . you're hungry. You're always hungry. Maybe you can think about how you abandoned me, instead of your stomach." Charlie spread the guilt on thick. "You can eat when we get back to camp. Until then, not another word." Chris handed Eli a bottle of water he got from his dad. Charlie was acting like a monster, but he wasn't going to let his kids go thirsty. Jack, on the other hand, would do without for the time being.

"So what now . . . Chuck?" Jack mocked. "You're just gonna wrangle a massive firebird and get rich?"

"I'd say that pretty much sums it up. No thanks to you, my job will be harder, but I'll get it done. Dead or alive."

"No thanks to me? If it weren't for me, Sam, and *your* boys, you wouldn't even know it exists."

"You were certainly trying to keep it that way, right?"

"I was waiting for the right time. We were still investigating and had to be sure what we were seeing. You were off 'chasing butterflies' and refused to believe anything we told you about the rock, the leaves, or the heart . . ." Jack faded off, knowing his words were falling on deaf ears.

"Like I said, I was wrong. I see that now. But it doesn't excuse you from your string of lies, and dragging my kids into it! Turning them against me!" Charlie barked in rage. Jack thought it futile to keep talking.

When they returned to the rock, Jack saw for the first time the destruction left behind. The flashes from the phoenix had charred the trees down to their trunks. Shadows were burned into the ground. It took an immense heat source to create those markings, yet no one got burned. A chunk of the tree near the cave was missing, imprinted with small holes, carved out by the blast from the gun. *If we had been standing two feet to the left . . .* Jack couldn't finish the thought.

The cave had burned out completely, the nest nothing more than ashes. Then Jack noticed it . . . *the heart. It's gone.* No imprint. No divot. No trace that it ever existed. With nothing left to see, Charlie pushed them forward. They walked through the second clearing without stopping, without another word.

Soon they filed back into camp. Eli released Popcorn from his confinement and beelined it for the rations, where they took solace in a bag of potato chips. Jack was imprisoned in his tent, but not before Charlie made Chris check it for anything that could be used as a weapon.

Before Jack went inside, he looked at Charlie with pure disgust. He was angrier than he ever thought possible, but knew better than to react in any way which would provoke his 'friend' any further.

Chris zipped up the flap on Jack's tent, enclosing him in his cell. Charlie even built an alarm system from some empty soda cans and silverware, tying it to the front of the tent to ensure any escape attempt would alert him.

"What now, Dad?" Chris asked. He didn't know what

to do with himself. He wanted to go out and search for Sam and Tommy.

"Now, we wait."

"Wait for what?"

"For Sam and your brother to return. They'll get hungry soon enough and make their way back. When they do, the phoenix will likely be close behind. When that happens, I will do whatever I have to."

"Please don't kill it, Dad. It's a living creature, something nobody thought existed in real life." Chris pleaded with Charlie, unsure his request would be heard, much less heeded.

"Like I said, I will do whatever is necessary. If that means the bird dies, then so be it. Dead or alive." Charlie's callousness in pursuit of glory left Chris defeated.

Chris wanted his dad back; the man he looked up to, the man who was kind and loving. He would have to wait. With the sun setting and the cold, humid air moving in, Chris retired to his tent, hopeful that Sam and his brother would be okay, hopeful that the phoenix would protect them and keep them warm.

CHAPTER FOURTEEN

S am and Tommy arrived back at the waterfall only to be disappointed. There was no sign of the phoenix.

"Ash!" Sam called out. "Ash! Help!" Nothing. She tried several more times, but the only response was the echo of her voice from deep in the canyon.

"He's not coming, Sam. What are we gonna do?"

"We need to keep going. Ash has to be around here somewhere."

They waded through the creek to the other side of the waterfall, continuing along the route, which soon started curving back toward the east. With the waning sun at their backs, Sam knew they needed to find shelter and food. They had less than an hour of sunlight remaining, and neither of them had a flashlight. Those were unfortunately left behind during the chaos at the boulder, although Sam still had her cell phone. She pulled it out of her pocket. *Dead.*

The crisp night air was already setting in. "It's getting cold. We need to find shelter and fast," said Sam.

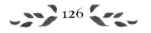

"Yeah, but where?"

"I think we should head back into the forest a little bit. Maybe there's another rock with a cave."

Tommy followed Sam away from the canyon, back under the dense shade of the woods. The deeper they hiked the darker it got, but it was their only option. Seeing was becoming increasingly difficult with every minute that passed, but no form of shelter was presenting itself. No rocks. No caves.

"We need to stop, Sam. I can barely see my hand in front of my face."

"Just a few more minutes. Stay close." Sam reached back and grabbed Tommy's hand. "Stay with me."

As they trudged forward in total darkness, their progress slowed considerably before coming to a full stop moments later. Sam relented, knowing they couldn't go any farther until morning. There was no ambient light to guide their way. It was a moonless night, and the clouds ensured that not even the brightest of stars could be seen above. A cold wind was picking up, letting the kids know they were in for a long night. Shivering and hungry, they lowered themselves to the ground. Sam pulled Tommy close, huddled against a tree, doing what was necessary to stay warm.

Two hours passed without a word spoken. They attempted to fall asleep, but the strangeness of their surroundings wouldn't allow it. Bizarre sounds echoed through the forest. Visions of movement all around them played tricks on their eyes, but nothing materialized. They remained intertwined, but the chilly air left them uncomfortable.

Then, as if by miracle, a familiar warm gust pushed its way through the trees. Sam and Tommy jumped to their feet just as Ash appeared and hovered overhead, providing the light and heat they desperately needed. "Ash!" Sam yelled in excitement.

With Ash above them, they could finally look around and take in their surroundings. Encircled by trees and bushes, they could not tell from which direction they had entered. Tommy took charge. "This way," he commanded.

Sam followed him as they pushed their way through a tall, thick briar of thorny bushes. A poke or scratch accompanied every step. "Tommy, where are we going?" Sam exclaimed with a wince as a large thorn poked the back of her hand.

"We're almost there. Keep going."

"Almost where? This hurts!" As she finished her words, they broke into a small clearing measuring only fifteen feet in diameter.

"Ash couldn't land back there. There were too many trees."

"So, you dragged us through that bush? Look at my hands and arms. Look at *your* hands and arms." They both had paper-thin scratches and pinpricks seeping blood. "What were you thinking?"

"I don't know. Something told me we had to go that way, so I went. I'm sorry."

Sam contemplated Tommy's choice of words, and then looked up to see the bird still above them. "It was Ash. He told you."

"What are you talking about? I didn't hear him say anything."

"Telepathy. Phoenixes can communicate with their minds. My mom told me about that, but I didn't remember it until now. Suddenly, it all makes sense. It's why I was able to talk to him earlier. I didn't realize it, but I understood him. And now you understand him too."

Sam and Tommy looked up at Ash. Slowly, he descended toward them, coming to rest on the ground and holding his wings halfway open, providing heat for the kids. It was as far as he could spread his massive wingspan within the tiny clearing.

"Hi there. Thank you for finding us. It's so cold out here," said Sam. The phoenix let out a series of small chirps.

"What did he say?"

"I'm not sure. I don't understand the sounds. I'm guessing he's saying, 'You're welcome'?

"Say it again, but this time only think it. Like telepathy."

Sam nodded and intently stared at Ash, locking eyes and trying to penetrate the giant bird's mind with her thoughts. *Hi there. Thank you for finding us.*

Ash, still locked in with Sam, responded with the same series of chirps as before, but this time Sam could hear something. A thought pushed into her mind. The voice she heard was her own, but Sam knew it was Ash responding.

You're welcome. Are you okay?

Sam answered without words. *Yes, but we're cold and hungry.*

Ash whistled and took off; his light quickly vanished, leaving them once again in darkness. "Wait. Where are you going?" yelled Tommy. "Sam, where is he going?"

"I don't know; he didn't say." The cold air quickly chilled them again. Sam and Tommy drew nearer to stay warm. Tommy reached out and put his arms around her, holding her close; he hoped not too close for her comfort. He only wanted to keep her warm and safe.

Within minutes, the sky brightened and Sam jumped back, pushing herself from Tommy's grasp. Ash had returned. In his beak were several twigs, each full of berries. *Eat,* he said to Sam, as he dropped the bounty to their feet.

Tommy, grateful for Ash's gift, attempted to respond. *Thank you, Ash.* He didn't hear a reply. He concentrated harder, squinted his eyes, and looked even more deeply at the phoenix, repeating himself, his facing contorting in the process. *Thank you, Ash.* Again, nothing. "How do you do it, Sam?"

"Well, for starters, I don't make those silly faces." She was laughing with a mouthful of berries. Tommy waved her off, realizing he was being made fun of, and turned his attention to the food in front of him. Ash once again spread his wings as far as the forest clearing would allow, basking Sam and Tommy in his warmth as they finished their meal. Sam looked to the bird. *We need to sleep. Will you stay and keep*

us warm?

Lie down and rest. I will keep you safe, Ash responded.

"He wants us to lie down, Tommy. He said he'd stay with us tonight so we can sleep."

Sam and Tommy proceeded to get on the ground. They lay with their heads near each other, their bodies in opposite directions. Each placed an arm tucked under their head and curled into a fetal position on their sides. Ash slowly pulled his wings around and under them, cradling the kids in a cocoon and pulling them into his fiery embrace; they could feel the softness of his feathers. Sam and Tommy raised their heads and looked at each other in awe of what was happening, and couldn't help but smile.

Rest your heads, Ash requested.

Sam began to translate for Tommy, but he immediately stopped her. "Rest your heads. I heard it," he whispered. "Goodnight, Sam."

"Goodnight, Tommy. Sleep tight." They both closed their eyes. As they did, Ash dimmed his light and began singing a low lullaby of coos and whistles, putting them to sleep immediately. They felt safe and secure. Once Ash finished his song, he tucked his head down into his wing closest to Sam and went to sleep as well.

Back at camp, Chris sat in his tent, wide awake. He couldn't sleep knowing Sam and Tommy were out there, without supplies or cover. His dad's words kept running through his mind, as well. *I'll do whatever I have to do. Dead or alive.* He knew he couldn't sit there and do nothing, but he was also worried about Eli, and even more concerned by what his dad might do to Jack. At least they were at camp. Sleeping. Fed. Safe . . . relatively speaking.

Chris quietly packed his sack with some water bottles, crackers, and a couple of apples and ninjaed his way out of camp, sneaking past Charlie's tent and down the path. Once out of sight, he turned on his flashlight and hurriedly made his way to the clearing. He took a moment to look around and gather his thoughts. *Stick to the path? Or create my own?* Chris trusted his sense of direction. The rock was due west. They had been moving south along the canyon when escaping from Charlie. He hoped that Sam and Tommy would have continued that direction, away from danger. He decided to trust his instinct and made his way through the forest in a southwesterly direction, hoping to cut them off. *They couldn't have gotten too far,* he thought.

For the next two hours, Chris pushed through the bushes and trees. The wilderness was unforgiving, putting giant boulders and impassable hedgerows in his way. He was no longer confident he was moving in the right direction, despite not meandering far off his original vector. Exhausted, he decided to stop and rest, despite his desire to find his brother and Sam. He sat down and propped himself against a tree. Before he realized it, his eyes drifted shut and he was dozing. He woke himself up with his own snoring. He checked his watch. *5:30? I was asleep for three hours?!* Chris sprang to his feet. He could see a dim light growing toward the east—*the sun.* Once again, he had his bearings. He corrected course and continued toward the southwest.

After hiking another thirty minutes, Chris still hadn't arrived at the cliff-edge as expected, but instead came to the banks of a shallow creek. He reached down to take a drink of water. It was ice cold, and just what was needed to keep going. He didn't dare eat what was in his pack; that was for Tommy and Sam. *They must be starving by now.*

Suddenly, Chris' thoughts were squelched by a deep growl behind him. He slowly turned around and found himself face to face with a mountain lion. It wasn't all that big, but he could see that it was sizing him up. It had likely been stalking him for some time, waiting for the right moment to attack its prey. It was rare for a mountain lion to attack a human, but they were unstoppable if hungry enough. This particular cat looked like it hadn't eaten much in a few weeks, its ribs protruding from its thin frame.

Chris put his hands up and began to back up slowly through the creek. The cold water shocked his skin through his shoes and pant legs, but he maintained eye-lock with his pursuer. The lion moved forward, matching Chris step for step, its growl turning to a loud, raspy scream. Chris was terrified and continued to back up, but before he knew it, he was on his back. He tripped over a stump and landed on the far edge of the creek embankment, his feet still in the water.

The cat made its move and pounced on top of him.

Chris fought back with all his might, grabbing the mountain lion's neck with both hands to keep from getting bit. Its teeth were menacing; it was determined to kill. It's powerful, razor-sharp claws swiped at Chris over and over, ripping through his arms, chest, and stomach. He wasn't sure how much longer he could keep up the fight, but he maintained his grip on its neck using all his remaining strength to try and choke the beast into submission. Unfortunately, his hands and arms were giving out, and the painful gashes he was enduring were taking their toll.

As his grip failed, the cat reared back on its hind legs to go in for the final blow, its sights aimed at Chris' throat. *FLASH, FLASH, FLASH.* Chris was blinded as suddenly, the weight of the mountain lion was no longer on him; he heard it whimper in pain. He quickly regained his focus, just in time to see his adversary running into the forest and out of sight. He then turned to see Tommy and Sam standing there, the phoenix by their side. That was when Chris passed out.

"Oh my gosh, Chris! Are you okay?" Tommy yelled, rushing to his side. His brother was bloody and didn't move, his shirt torn to shreds, his wounds critical.

Move aside young one, Ash said calmly to Tommy. But Tommy didn't budge, not wanting to leave Chris' side.

"He said . . ." Sam couldn't finish.

"I know, I heard. Move away," Tommy said solemnly, worried about his brother. He looked up at Ash and begrudgingly complied, moving back slowly.

Ash hopped toward Chris, positioning himself at his

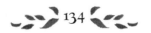

feet. As he did, his tail feathers fell into the cold creek water, and steam began to rise. Ash raised his wings high over his head, the tips of each wing meeting at the top. Then the phoenix bent over, sweeping his wings down over Chris' injured body. Sam and Tommy watched as Chris disappeared beneath the wings. They said nothing, uncertain of what they were watching, but they trusted that the bird was trying to help. Ash remained still with his wings draped over Chris' body as steam filled the air around them.

A few minutes later, the phoenix pulled its fiery feathers back and tucked them behind its body. Ash hopped back toward Sam and Tommy. *He must rest now*, Ash conveyed to them.

Sam and Tommy walked over to Chris, astonished by what they saw. He was still lying on the ground. "Is he . . . ?" Sam was unsure.

He's asleep and must rest to regain his strength, Ash replied.

Tommy looked down on his brother's seemingly lifeless body. Aside from a bloody and tattered shirt, Chris showed no sign of injury. "His cuts . . . they're gone!" Tommy said in disbelief. "How?"

"The myth is real. Ash healed him," Sam answered. She looked down at her own hands and arms, cut by the thorny bushes the night before. *Nothing. Not even a scratch or a scar.* "Tommy, look." She held out her arms in display. Tommy glanced down to notice that he, too, was healed. Once again, Ash had saved them, and now he had mended their wounds.

They weren't sure how long Chris needed to rest. They

were just happy he was alive and well. Sam and Tommy made their way back to Ash and nestled into his body to wait. Sam grabbed his wing and pulled it up over her like a blanket. *Thank you, Ash. You're amazing,* she told him. He responded with a chirp and a coo, then began to sing the same lullaby from the night before. It brought them comfort.

CHAPTER FIFTEEN

Where am I?" Chris muttered, his eyes still half shut. "What happened?" He attempted to sit up but quickly fell back, still weak from his encounter with the mountain lion. He had been unconscious for almost an hour.

You're safe now, but you need to rest, Ash transmitted.

Chris was still dazed and trying to regain his composure. "Huh? Who said that?" Rubbing his eyes back into focus, he turned to see Sam and Tommy. "What did you say?"

"We didn't say anything. Ash did," said Tommy.

"Who did?" Chris asked as he finally sat up and caught sight of the massive bird. His eyes widened, coming face to face with the phoenix for the first time.

"Chris, meet Ash," introduced Sam.

Are you feeling better? Chris squinted at Ash, still trying to understand what was going on.

"You . . . ? But how . . . ?" He was at a loss for words.

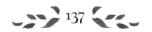

"Telepathy. We can hear him too," Sam replied, helping him fill in the blanks.

You had quite the experience, Ash continued.

"I'd say I still am," Chris said in amazement. "Wow . . . this is incredible. You saved me. I saw the flashes, but that's all I remember."

"That big bad cat almost got you, bro. Ash scared it off and then fixed you up." Tommy pointed to Chris' tattered and blood-stained shirt.

Chris looked down at his torso and arms, astonished by what he was seeing. Not even a scratch. "How is that possible?"

"He's a phoenix. He can heal," Sam interjected. "That's what he does."

"But . . ." Chris stuttered, still trying to force logic into the situation.

Like she said, it's what I do, Ash proclaimed. *Though not all I do.*

Sam and Tommy giggled at the phoenix's sense of humor, though not convinced it was on purpose. Ash let out a short melody of chirps, imitating the kids as if laughing with them. It caused them to laugh even more.

Chris waited for the laughter to die down. He was yearning for answers. "Why are you here? Where did you come from?"

Ash told his story to the kids, verifying the myth that Sam had come to love thanks to her mom. His thousand years in Paradise had come to an end. He chose this area to die and

be reborn due to the magical qualities contained in the surrounding rocks. Arizona was the site of well-known vortices—swirling pockets of mystical, healing energy. Native Americans believed spiritual transformation was attainable here.

Phoenixes used these natural phenomena to harness the power needed to transform and rise from their ashes. Over the millennia, Ash had performed his ritual in many areas of the world, from the pyramids of Egypt to Stonehenge and Ayers Rock in Australia, each time visiting one of these powerful centers of intense energy. The last time Ash had come to the mortal realm, one thousand years earlier, he had chosen Haleakala, the volcano on the Hawaiian island of Maui.

"When are you going to transform?" asked Sam. She knew it would be soon, but didn't want to see Ash leave yet.

I've been attempting to for the past few days, but without any luck. I built the nest under the rock with the heart in hopes of transforming, but it wasn't meant to be.

The heart, Sam thought. "There's a vortex there! That's why the leaves swirled when we touched the heart!" Ash whistled and chirped in concurrence. Sam continued, "Then why couldn't you transform?"

Perhaps the energy there isn't strong enough. I'm over eight thousand years old. Every transformation requires more energy than the last, but I have never failed to transform.

Sam and Jack hadn't been in Arizona long, but she was already familiar with the vortexes of Sedona. "I think I know how to help. The red rocks back home are famous for their vortex powers. They make me dizzy every time I'm near them, especially Bell Rock. It's about two hours from here. We need to go!"

"But how are we gonna get there?" Chris chimed in. "Our dad still has your dad under watch."

"He's a phoenix, he can just fly there, duh," Tommy imparted sarcastically.

You are still in danger. I cannot risk leaving you alone, even if it means being trapped in this world and dying as a mortal creature.

"What are you talking about, Ash? I thought phoenixes were immortal. You die and are reborn in three days." Sam was defensive at the thought of Ash not being able to carry out his destiny.

Yes, you are correct, we are immortal, but only in my realm, in Paradise. The ritual must take place during the new moon, or I will not be able to return. I will die of old age in your world if I cannot complete my thousand-year cycle. The new moon will wax toward a crescent in two days. But I am bound to protect human life. Your safety and your lives come before my own.

"We need to get you to Sedona. I'm not going to let you get stuck here and die." Sam's thoughts betrayed her. She wanted to have Ash around forever. She didn't want him to go back to Paradise. *He saved me. I need to save him.* She wouldn't let her selfish needs get in the way of helping Ash complete his sacrament.

"If we can get back to camp and get the keys, I can drive

us," Chris offered.

"You know how to drive?" Sam asked.

"I mean, not well, but I've been learning."

Sam searched for another option, but nothing was coming to mind. "I suppose we don't have much choice."

"So that's it? We sneak back into camp and steal Dad's truck? Foolproof," Tommy said cynically.

"Do you have a better idea, butthead?" Tommy fell silent. "That's what I thought."

"We need to move fast. Ash doesn't have much time." Sam was ready to spring into action even if their plan was a bit roughshod.

Ready to make their return, a familiar voice came echoing through the trees. "Chris, where are you? Chris! Tommy!" It was Charlie. He repeated himself, his voice getting louder, growing nearer.

"We need to go now," Chris commanded, grabbing his sack. "Ash, go! Hide! Dad cannot find you. He said he'll kill you." They began to move swiftly downriver and back toward the canyon as Ash took off through the trees and out of sight.

Moments later, two gunshots rang out. *BOOM. BOOM.* Sam stopped in her tracks, but Tommy immediately grabbed her by the hand to keep her moving forward. "He'll be fine, we need to keep going."

As they approached the cliff edge, Charlie's voice grew dimmer. They were gaining distance, but had to keep moving. They followed the canyon as it veered east along an animal path. Chris hoped it was just deer and not another beastly meat-eater. Despite the distance they had put between themselves and danger, they kept pushing forward, but after another thirty minutes, Sam decided they could afford a quick break.

"I need to stop. Just for a minute. Please. I'm so tired."

"Are you okay?" Tommy was worried. He knew Sam wanted to keep going and wouldn't stop if she didn't have to.

Chris reached into his bag and grabbed an apple and some water. "Here, this should help. I think we've got some time. Sit and rest. Eat."

Sam sat down on a fallen tree with its roots exposed, suspended over the canyon wall like a wooden waterfall. Tommy took a seat next to her, hip-to-hip, putting his arm around her shoulder. "You know he's okay, right?" She nodded, taking a bite from the apple. Tommy tried his best to console her. "Have faith. Ash helped us, and now we get to help him."

"Guys, check this out," Chris called. Sam and Tommy pushed their way off the log and followed Chris one hundred feet down the trail to a rock jutting out over the canyon. From here, the canyon turned north-northeast. They climbed out to the perilous point, being careful not to get too close to the edge. Chris pointed to the far side of the canyon. "There . . . do you see it? On the other side of the canyon?"

In the far distance was a familiar site to Sam. *The cave and waterfall.* "I know where we are. Dad and I saw that cave on our hike the other day. There's a switchback trail that leads to the bottom of the canyon. We can't be too far from there. If we can get there, we'll find the path back to camp."

"I guess we have a plan," Chris said approvingly. "Show us the way, young padawan." Sam rolled her eyes and pushed Chris aside as she jumped ahead to take the lead.

They followed the canyon rim, which forced them north. The terrain began to ease up and allowed the kids to move quite a bit faster than before, the cave and waterfall getting closer all the time. Before long they reached the trail, and Ash waiting there to greet them.

"Ash, are you okay?" Sam said worriedly. "We heard the gunshots."

Not a scratch, my dear.

"We're headed back to get the truck. Once we have it, follow us to Bell Rock," Sam requested.

"Is that the best idea?" questioned Tommy. "What if someone sees him? That's a pretty long drive . . . or in his case, flight, to go unseen."

"You're right, but he's too big to fit in the bed of the truck," Sam stated.

Not to rush, but I noticed your dad on his way back to the camp. You will need to hurry, explained Ash.

Chris retook the lead, "Let's go. We'll figure it out later. Right now, we just need to beat Dad back and get the truck."

CHAPTER SIXTEEN

Sam, Tommy, and Chris bounded into the campground, ready to grab the keys and get Ash to safety, but Charlie had other plans. "Welcome back," he said sarcastically. "Having fun yet?" Charlie still had the gun in his hand. Eli sat silently near the fire pit, trying to stay out of his dad's way, fearful of his wrath.

"Where's my Dad?" Sam questioned.

Jack's voice boomed from his tent. "In here, Princess. I'm fine." Sam noticed the makeshift alarm hanging from his tent.

"Let him go! Now!" she demanded.

"Your daddy will be staying right where he is. No one is gonna hurt him." Charlie's malicious smile made Sam think otherwise.

She continued her demand. "I want to see him."

"Go right ahead, sweetheart, but don't try anything funny." As Sam raced to her dad, Charlie turned his attention to Chris and Tommy. "You boys have something to say for

yourselves? Y'all came storming in here like you had something important to do. Care to explain?" Charlie turned his attention back to Jack's tent, to ensure Sam wasn't getting away with anything. "I'm listening," he told the boys.

Tommy loved his dad, but he knew he had to speak up. "We need to save A . . . the phoenix. He needs to transform, or he'll die."

"Transform? And how would you know this? Did he tell you this? That big bird talk to you?" Charlie mocked his son's response.

Chris started to speak up in Tommy's defense, but got cut off. "Yes, he did tell me," Tommy bravely answered. "He told all of us. He needs our help."

Charlie burst into laughter. "You've told some pretty tall tales, but this one takes the cake, son. I mean, the fact that this thing is real is still blowing my mind, but it talks too?" He looked at Chris. "You too?" Chris nodded his head in silence; any verbal response would have undoubtedly been met with ridicule and derision. Charlie couldn't control his laughter.

Sam pushed aside Charlie's contraption and opened her dad's tent. Instantly, she noticed that his wrists were bound. Jack could see the look of horror on her face. "Dad!" She reached out and hugged him tight. "Are you okay?"

"My wrists are a little sore, but otherwise I'm fine."

"Back up and stay where I can see you," Charlie yelled to Sam.

She loosened her grip on her dad and retreated to the

entrance of the tent. "We need to get Ash out of here. He's in danger, and not just from Charlie," she whispered.

"Ash? The phoenix?"

Sam nodded her head. "We need to get him back home. To our home . . . so that he can go back to his." She was stumbling, struggling to get her dad to understand. There was so much to say, but she was worried Charlie would pull her away at any moment. She stopped momentarily to gather her thoughts and take a deep breath. "He can't transform here. He needs the power of the Bell Rock vortex. We were coming to get the truck and show him the way."

"Wait, did I hear correctly? Did Tommy say it could talk? That it told you this?"

"Through telepathy, yes," she affirmed.

Jack smiled in excitement. "Princess, that's incredible. I want to get out of here and help you, but as long as Charlie has that gun . . ." Jack trailed off, unsure what they could do.

"Ash will help us. I think I have an idea how. Stay here."

Raising his wrists, Jack responded, "I'll be here." Sam scurried to her feet. "Princess?" he called to Sam. She bent down to listen. "Be careful. If anything goes wrong, get far away from here and away from him. I love you."

"I love you too, Dad. I'll get you out of here really soon. I promise."

Sam rejoined Chris and Tommy, now sitting with Eli and Popcorn by the cold, ash-filled campfire. Charlie yelled out from his tent across camp, "I've got my eye on you, bird whisperer," he said threateningly to Sam.

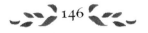

Sam gave Charlie an ironic thumbs-up, ignoring his wicked glare. She turned to the boys. "Change of plans," she whispered. "As long as your dad has that gun, we're stuck here. I doubt he's gonna let us out of our tents come nightfall. We need to get Ash to cause a distraction so we can escape."

"How do we find him, though? He's always found us," asked Tommy.

"We talk to him. The same way we have been. I'm not sure how far away he can hear our thoughts, but maybe if we all try at the same time, it'll work. He's likely not too far away," Sam guessed.

"Okay, then what?" Chris asked.

"If we can get your dad away from camp, then we can make a run for it. But not without my dad. As soon as it's clear, both of you will need to find a knife. Tommy, I need you to cut my dad free. Chris, I'll need you to slash the tires on your dad's truck so he can't follow us." Both boys nodded.

"What about me?" Eli said, wanting in on the plan. Popcorn clicked his teeth, wanting a piece of the action as well.

"You have the most important job . . . get both sets of truck keys. Can you do that? We need to make sure there's no way your dad can follow us. My dad's keys are in the glove box." Eli nodded. "Once everyone does their job, we meet back at the truck."

"What's your job?" Tommy queried.

"I'm going for the ammo. We might not be able to pry the gun away from your dad, but it won't do him any good if he's out of bullets."

"He keeps the shotgun shells in a box in the cab of his truck," Chris said. "He probably has two in the gun and two more in his pocket, but we won't know for sure until we get that box. By my count, he's already used four shells; two at the rock and two in the forest."

Sam looked at each of the boys. "You guys ready for this? We only have one shot at making it work. Ash is counting on us. So is my dad." They all nodded. Sam looked over her shoulder to see where Charlie was. *Still by his tent fiddling with something.* "Here goes nothing. Concentrate on Ash. Let him know what we need."

The four kids all closed their eyes, sending their message out into the late afternoon sky. They waited, but nothing happened. Again they closed their eyes, focusing harder. They waited, but still nothing. "I'm not sure he can hear us, Sam," Tommy said dejectedly.

"Try again. We can't stop until it works," Sam demanded. "Now, close your eyes and . . ."

Sam's commands were interrupted by a stream of warm air pushing past them. They immediately looked up to see Ash circling above. Sam directed her attention to Charlie, who had already popped to his feet, gun in hand.

He cocked the gun. "Here little birdy birdy," he called, followed by a whistle. He aimed skyward.

Sam looked back to Ash, who swiftly flew toward the rock as the gunshot boomed and echoed; she could feel the compression in her chest. *He missed.* Without a thought for anyone else, Charlie fled the camp, chasing after the phoenix.

"Go! Now!" Sam commanded. "Hurry!"

Everyone sprang into action, scared but focused on the tasks at hand. Tommy quickly found a knife, freed Jack, and they made their way to the truck. The unmistakable hiss of a tire sinking to the ground could be heard. Sam could feel the truck getting lower as she grabbed the box of ammo and scoured the truck cab, making sure she accounted for every shell.

BOOM. Another blast rang out in the distance. Sam would have to push her worry to the back of her mind until they reached safety.

Eli was the first to speak amidst the chaos. "The keys aren't here!" he shouted, jumping down from the cab of Jack's truck.

Jack responded in haste, "They're in his tent. He took them earlier."

"Why didn't you say something, Eli?" Chris asked incredulously.

"I didn't know," he said, frustrated and sad that he wasn't able to complete his mission.

"Too busy stuffing your face?" reprimanded Chris, as he ran across camp to retrieve the keys.

"Stop! We don't have time for this. Just get the keys," said Sam. "Everyone else, get in the truck." Complying with her orders, Jack jumped into the driver seat. Tommy and Eli jumped in the bed of the truck while Sam stayed poised, waiting for Chris to return.

Chris seemed to be taking a long time finding the keys,

prompting Sam to run over and help him. Before she could get a word in edgewise, Chris cried out, "They're not here! He must've taken them with him."

"Keep looking," Sam replied, joining the search. They began turning the tent upside down, desperate to find the keys. Just as they were about to give up, Popcorn bounded into the tent and started sniffing around. Within seconds, the clever ring-tail poked his head from beneath the sleeping bag, keys in mouth.

"Good job, little guy! Let's go!" said Chris.

When they got back to the truck, Sam threw Jack the keys and jumped in, Chris joining her in the cab. "These aren't my keys," Jack responded.

"What?" Sam replied.

"These are Charlie's keys."

"They were the only ones we could find," Chris said, now fearing their plan was falling apart.

"What's going on? Why aren't we leaving?" Tommy yelled from the bed.

BOOM. A third shot, this one closer than the last. Charlie was on his way back.

"We need to go," said Jack.

As they piled from the truck, Sam glanced down at the flat tire, realizing the keys in hand were useless. "I know where we can go. Follow me!" Sam quickly headed toward the trail that led back to the canyon. "Let's go!" Everyone followed, not waiting around to question her judgment. If they didn't leave immediately, Charlie would be back for

them. Only a few hundred yards down the path, Sam stopped everyone. "We need to go back. I forgot the shells. We can't let your dad get them," she said fearfully to Chris.

Tommy swung the backpack off his shoulder and opened it—he had grabbed it during their hasty retreat. "These shells?" he mentioned pridefully, presenting the box to Sam.

Sam couldn't contain her relief. She grabbed Tommy and hugged him tight. "Oh my God, you're amazing! Thank you!" She kissed him on the cheek. Tommy blushed a shade of crimson, nearing purple. Popcorn stuck his tongue out as if gagging in disgust.

"Ahem," Jack said, feigning a throat clearing.

Chris chimed in, "I second that. We don't have time for all this mushy stuff."

Sam, too, was now blushing. Trying to break the awkwardness, she turned her back from the group and continued down the trail. "Follow me." A smile crossed her face that no one else could see, that she didn't want anyone else to see.

Chris pulled up the rear of the pack, placing a hand on Tommy's head and messing his hair. "Let's go, loverboy." Still embarrassed, Tommy swatted Chris' hand away.

The group picked up the pace, trying to distance themselves from Charlie. When they reached the canyon edge, the waterfall came into view. The setting sun sparked a colorful display across the far canyon wall, a misty rainbow pointing to the cave. "There. We'll be safe there," Sam said.

Without a word from the others, Sam started down the steep trail across the face of the cliff. They zig-zagged their way two hundred feet to the bottom of the canyon. By the time they finished their descent, dusk had settled, making it difficult to see.

On cue as always, Ash swooped in to provide the light they needed. Hopping from rock to rock, they made it across the river to the mouth of the cave. The waterfall blanketed the entrance and covered them in a fine spray as water bounced off the rocks nearby.

After you, Ash said. As he opened his wings wide, the curtain of water separated, creating a dry archway for them to enter the cave. They all stood there, stunned. They knew Ash had magical powers, but this was one that not even Sam had known. Her mom would have been equally mystified.

One by one they filed into the cave, taking time to look above at the water suspended in place, astonished but dry. Once inside, Ash joined them, letting the waterfall resume its cascade and keeping them safe within. Thanks to Ash, the cave was well lit.

The ceiling soared over fifty feet high and was lined with stalactites ominously holding on from above. A small stream of water meandered down the center of the cavern, pushing one hundred feet deep, fed by groundwater soaking through the rock. It was cathedral-like, and Ash's light provided a stained glass effect of dancing colors on the limestone walls.

Sam was awestruck, but quickly fell to her knees,

grabbing her head with both hands. "Princess, what's wrong?" Jack rushed to her side.

"I'm dizzy, and my head hurts." She tried to stand back up, but Jack refused, seeing that she was not well.

"Stay down for a few," he requested.

There's a strong vortex here, that's why you're not feeling well. You are rare, Sam. You mentioned your sensitivity, but until now, I did not realize how special you are. Not many in the mortal realm have such strong reactions to these forces. These energies only choose those who are worthy of being able to harness their powers. You must learn to control them and use them for good.

Chris spoke up, saying what was now on everyone's mind. "You're saying Sam has magical powers?"

Everyone does to some extent, but they lack the ability to tap into them. Sam, however, has powers beyond most. I wish I could stay and help her learn to control them, but once my transformation is complete, I will have to return to Paradise. Sedona is home to many practitioners because of the vortexes. Sam, you will have to seek out a teacher worthy of guiding you.

Sam nodded, still holding her head in one hand and trying to regain her focus. She slowly stood up, Tommy at her elbow to keep her steady. "If what you're saying is true, then this place has the strength for you to complete your transformation." Ash cooed and whistled. "We don't have time to waste then. How can we help?"

I must build a nest and gather all the ingredients necessary to ensure I can be reborn in three days. I will need to collect primrose, toadflax, and blackberries. The nest must be created from branches of the Tree of Heaven. All of these items are nearby.

"Aside from the blackberries, I'm not sure any of us know what the other items look like," Jack said.

"I do," Eli said meekly. "We learned about plants in scouts. I can help find the primrose and toadflax, but I've never heard of that heaven tree before."

"Perfect!" Jack exclaimed. "Chris, you take Eli and gather the primrose and toadflax. Tommy, Sam, and I will find the blackberries. Ash, if you can get the tree branches you need, then we can have your nest built before sunrise. Keep a low profile and be as quiet as possible. Everyone needs to be back here in one hour, even if you didn't finish gathering everything."

Armed with their flashlights, they set out to do their work. Jack, Sam, and Tommy headed north along the river. Ash flew north as well, staying below the top of the canyon walls, while Chris and Eli headed south.

Charlie watched from above.

CHAPTER SEVENTEEN

It had been nearly an hour. Jack, Sam, and Tommy approached the waterfall, waiting for Ash to return and create a dry entrance for them to cross. They flicked off their flashlights to avoid drawing any unnecessary attention. "Where are Chris and Eli?" Tommy whispered.

"I don't know, but I hope they show up soon. We need to get the nest built," Jack replied.

Sam turned her light back on and looked south down the dark river valley, but there were no signs of them. "We can't wait much longer. We need to go find them," she worriedly exclaimed. As she finished her sentence, a light came up from behind them, illuminating the entire canyon. *Ash.* They all turned to greet him as he came to rest on a large boulder, his beak full of branches from the Tree of Heaven. But something wasn't right. Sam immediately noticed the darkness of his colors. "What's wrong?" she asked.

They're in the cave, and they're not alone, he responded.

"Charlie?!" Sam cried out in disbelief.

An echo rang out from behind the sheet of water. "You looking for me, little one?"

Ash dropped the branches, spread his wings, and parted the waters revealing the cave behind. Chris and Eli were seated on the ground with their haul of primrose and toadflax scattered around them. Charlie stood waiting, gun in hand. All three soaked from their trek through the falling water.

"Put the gun down, Charlie," Jack pleaded. "There's no need for this."

"I'll be the one making the demands here. Now get in the cave," Charlie said, using the gun to motion them in.

Sam looked back at Ash, scared and unsure. *Go. Do what he says. But keep your ears and mind open,* he answered, anticipating how Sam was feeling and not needing to hear her pending question.

Charlie's gun was still trained on them as they made their way into the cave. They passed the barrier of the water and before anyone could react, the wall of water resumed flowing, and Ash flashed out of sight. Charlie, unable to get off a shot, clutched his gun tight, mad that his prize had gotten away once again. Sam was thankful, but frightened.

With the cave pitched into total darkness, Charlie turned on his flashlight. "Everyone on the ground, now!" They inched their way to the cold, wet ground near Chris and Eli and complied; Popcorn too, covering his eyes with his paws. "So, here we are, yet again." Charlie's penchant for hearing himself speak was growing old, but they were in no place to protest. "My sons, my friend, and his little brat. Traitors! Do you think you can keep this secret from the world? This is the discovery of our lifetimes, and you'd rather protect that thing. Do you have any idea what kind of riches you're giving up? You'd be famous! We will all be famous. We've worked our entire careers for this, Jack. We've placed everything on the line for this moment. We've lost everything. My Diana. Your wife."

"Don't you dare mention my mother! She was sick!" Sam screamed at him, livid that he would use her mother's death to justify their previous lack of success.

"Yes, she was, darling. You think maybe that had something to do with the fact that your daddy was so focused on his work that he couldn't properly take care of her?" Charlie's lies and conspiracies were blatant, but no less painful. Sam began to sob at the thought of her deceased mother. She knew Jack had done everything he could to take care of Nan and make her comfortable until the end. It was never his fault.

Charlie laughed at Sam, mocking her grief. The echoes of his malice filled the cave and swarmed Sam's head. She wanted it to stop.

Through the reverberations of his cackle, Sam could hear a message pushing through. *Get on the ground and cover your eyes.* She immediately looked to the others, their eyes confirming they had heard Ash as well, even Jack. Collectively, they all dropped to their sides and covered their eyes. Before Charlie could question them, a continuous series of flashes filled the cave. Even with their eyes covered, they could feel and see the heat and the light. A rush of hot, moist air consumed them. *BOOM.* Charlie's gun discharged. Their ears rang from the blast as it echoed through the chamber. *FLASH, FLASH, FLASH.* Charlie had missed his mark.

Sam took the chance to open her eyes, hoping not to be blinded by any more flashes, but she could barely make out the others next to her. Ash had flown through the waterfall, creating a wake of thick fog. She now understood why Charlie missed his shot. The cave had filled with steam, the only light being a haze coming from Charlie's flashlight, which now lay on the ground. Sam scrambled to grab the light, confident that if she could get to it, Charlie would be completely blind.

Jack, with his head still buried in the crux of his arm, could feel Sam moving. "Sam, get back here. Where are you going?" He pulled his head up just in time to see the light extinguish. "Sam!" he yelled. But she offered no response.

Within seconds, Jack felt something brush his leg. "Shh, Dad. I'm fine," she whispered as she returned to the others.

They all remained quietly still, fearful of Charlie's next move. A growl from Eli's stomach finally broke the eerie silence. Jack realized that it had been silent for too long. No more flashes, no more gunshots. *Ash and Charlie are both gone,* he thought.

"You're right, Dad, they are," Sam responded, flipping on the flashlight. They both realized in that moment that she could hear her dad, despite that he hadn't spoken his

thoughts. They didn't ponder it long, as Chris turned on his flashlight as well.

"Where's my dad? Where's Ash?" The steam was starting to clear, and it was apparent that they were no longer under watch. Charlie's expended gun rested on the cave floor, a spent shell nearby.

"He saved us again!" Sam said with a little too much joy.

"But, where is our dad?" Chris asked again, sounding concerned and a little annoyed by Sam's lack thereof.

"I'm sure he's fine, son," Jack responded. "Ash won't hurt him. Phoenixes will not harm humans. They are life givers, not life takers." Chris nodded, knowing that Jack was right but he worried nonetheless, and was anxious about his dad's location.

"What now?" Tommy asked.

Sam was quick to reply. "We need to get the nest built for Ash. I know he'll be back."

They all began to gather the scattered ingredients, except for Chris, who solemnly walked to the front of the cave, still bothered by Charlie's disappearance. "Where are you going?" asked Eli.

"To find Dad. I need to know that he's safe."

"We need your help here, Chris. I promise after Ash transforms, we will all help you find Charlie and get him help." Sam begged, but Chris continued without a word, walking through the waterfall and disappearing on the other side. "Someone should go with him," she suggested.

Tommy spoke up first. "I'll go. I'll do my best to get him to come back. Just keep working on the nest."

Eli solemnly joined his brothers. "I'll go too. Dad needs our help." Popcorn mimicked Eli's mood with a sad whimper.

Jack and Sam nodded, knowing they wouldn't be able to change the boys' minds. "Just promise you'll be careful. And if there's any trouble, get back to camp and wait for us," Jack instructed. Tommy nodded in agreement.

Sam approached Tommy, wrapped her arms around him, and squeezed. "Be safe, Tommy." As she let go of her grip, she reached into her pocket and pulled her cherished heart-shaped stone from her pocket and handed it to him. "For luck." Tommy remained stoic despite the flutter he felt and responded with a wry, crooked smile. With his brother in tow, they turned and walked through the waterfall to chase down Chris and find their father. Sam stood there for a moment, hoping they would immediately turn around and come back to help build Ash's nest. She turned away, disappointed.

"Let's go, Princess. Let's get this nest built so it's ready when Ash returns." Jack tried to refocus Sam's heartbroken, defeated energy. "Why don't you gather all the items in the cave? I'll go get the branches."

Sam snapped out of her brief funk, realizing what needed to be done. She sprung to action and immediately set about putting together the nest. Unsure if there was a particular way to build it, they stacked the damp wood in layers to create a base, followed by the primrose and toadflax.

Finally, they placed the blackberries in the center. "I guess that should do it," Sam surmised.

"I hope it's to Ash's liking," Jack added. "We'll find out soon enough, I suppose."

With nothing left to do but wait for Ash's return, Sam grew restless, pacing back and forth, sighing with every turn. "Can we go look for the boys? Who knows how long we'll have to wait."

"Are you sure you don't want to be here when Ash gets back? If we leave and aren't back by sunrise, you'll miss your chance to say goodbye. I'd hate to see that happen. Besides, the boys will be fine." Jack tried reasoning with her. They had endured so much in the past few days, and he knew she'd regret not seeing Ash off.

"Ash has his nest, but the boys need our help. Charlie needs our help." Jack couldn't believe what she was saying, but he was proud of her. Despite the terror Charlie had caused them, she still saw the human side of the situation. Charlie was a man who was hurting and scared, and he needed their help.

"You're sure about this?"

Sam nodded.

They exited the cold shower of the waterfall, shining their flashlights through the canyon, hopeful for any sign of the boys, but there was none. There were no signs of Ash, either. Cold and wet, they slowly made their way up the cliff-side trail and back toward camp, optimistic that the boys and Charlie had already returned. Sam spent almost the entire hike with her neck craned skyward, on the lookout for her fiery friend. She concentrated, sending out messages in hopes he would appear. *Ash, where are you? Where did you go? We need your help!* But her pleas went unanswered. She started to worry that perhaps Charlie had gotten the best of him.

Upon entering camp, it was clear that no one had returned. Jack and Sam made their way to their tents to get changed, knowing that any further searching in their sopping clothes and shoes would only make things harder. As they finished getting dressed and made their way out of their quarters, a bright light came over the camp from the west. Ash had returned, coming to rest on top of Charlie's now unusable truck. Seeing that Jack and Sam were cold, he ignited the campfire for them with the flick of a wing.

"Where's Charlie? What happened?" Sam questioned aloud.

He's safe. I left him at the clearing, unharmed. I led the boys to him, and they are with him now. They're heading back. We should return to the cave before they get here. Morning light is less than two hours from now.

"I think we should wait for them," Sam said. "He's not armed anymore. I think we should try and show him how special you are; why you're not some lost treasure he can turn in for a reward. Please, Ash. I know we're running out of time, but he needs to know. Charlie must be a good man, or my dad wouldn't have kept him as a friend all these years. He deserves another chance."

"Princess, I'm not sure there's time. Ash needs to get to

the cave." Jack was once bitten, twice shy after Charlie's shenanigans, and unconvinced they'd be able to get through to him, armed or otherwise.

"Dad, please. Have faith. He's your friend. He needs your help more than ever." Jack lowered his shoulders, relenting to his daughter's wisdom and pressure.

There's little time, Sam, but I will honor your request. You won't have a second to lose.

In a matter of minutes, the sound of the boys and Charlie made its way into camp. No voices, only the unmistakable sounds of leaves crunching and dragging feet. As they emerged through the trees, Charlie's rage took center stage. "You!" he yelled, pointing at Ash. "You tried to kill me! That damn bird is dangerous. It picked me up and took me to the clearing to kill me. It was about to disembowel me when the boys showed up and stopped it."

"Dad, that's not . . ." Tommy tried to interject the truth but was swiftly cut off.

"It tried to kill me, and now I'm going to kill it!" Charlie picked up the only weapon he could scrounge, a softball size rock, and charged at Ash. The phoenix stood his ground, opening and fanning his wings, ready to take off if needed. His colors deepened to a dark purple, almost black.

"No!" yelled Sam.

But before Charlie could reach his intended target, he was tackled to the ground. It was Chris. He laid on top of his dad, straddling him and pinning him down. Charlie didn't move. "Stop it, now, Dad! Ash is not yours. He's not anybody's!" Charlie still didn't move; his eyes were open and glazed over.

"Dad, are you hearing me?" Charlie remained motionless without a response. The rock trickled out of his hand. "Dad? . . . DAD!"

Chris moved off of Charlie and to his side. The others quickly gathered around. A pool of blood was growing below Charlie's head, as everyone realized what had happened. Charlie was gone. Eli and Tommy began to sob, as did Sam. Jack leaned down and closed Charlie's eyes. As he did, he could see the tent spike that had pierced the base of Charlie's neck. It was a horrific accident that no one could have predicted.

Sam looked up to Ash and, without a word, made clear her wish. "Get back," she demanded. "Everyone get back." The boys were reluctant to move in their grief, but quickly complied as Ash hopped forward toward Charlie's lifeless body. Ash scooped Charlie into his wings, lifting him slightly off the ground. The tent stake dropped to the ground, out of sight from the group. Ash laid Charlie back down and covered him with his wings, as he had done with Chris after the mountain lion attack. The blackness of his feathers soon glowed a multitude of colors and lit up the camp in a dancing rainbow of light too bright for them to look at directly. They all shielded their eyes as Ash's shine grew to a crescendo, then *FLASH!*

When the bright white light subsided and camp settled back into the darkness of night, Charlie still lay there as

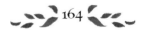

before. Ash flew into the distant, soft glow of the morning light, headed toward the cave.

"Dad?" Chris said, rushing to Charlie's side. There was no response. "Dad, wake up!" he yelled. Charlie did not respond. Chris grabbed his dad and buried his head in his chest, holding him, crying and shaking. An inconsolable Tommy and Eli joined him.

Sam turned to Jack and held on tight. She was in disbelief. *Ash was supposed to heal him. How could this be?* Popcorn mournfully crept toward Charlie, licked his cheek, and quickly retreated. The sound of coughing startled the animal into leaping behind Eli for safety. Sam lifted her head from Jack's embrace to see Charlie gasping for air.

"Dad! Dad!" Tommy yelled. "You're alive!"

Chris held on to Charlie tight, astonished that he was breathing, not sure if it was real. "Dad?"

Charlie let out one more cough before answering, "What happened?" He looked around, noticing the tears on their faces. "What's going on?"

Chris choked on his words and Jack quickly interjected. "You tripped and fell. You hit your head. You were gone."

"Gone? Gone where?"

"You died, Dad," replied Tommy.

"But, I'm right here. What are you saying?"

Sam spoke up. "He brought you back to life. Ash saved you . . . just like he saved Chris."

"Ash? The phoenix? But where is it?" Charlie struggled, trying to put two and two together.

"He's gone," Sam continued. "He's headed to the cave to complete his transformation. I'm glad you're okay, but I can't let you stop him, Charlie. Ash needs to transform. It's the only way he can stay alive. It's his only chance to be reborn and save others. He saved you, despite all the bad things you said and did. He saved you. He saved your son. Now do you believe?"

Charlie, still laying in Chris' arms, sat up. He grabbed the back of his neck. It was sore and bloody, but there was no wound. "He saved me," Charlie said solemnly, repeating Sam's words. "He saved my life. I . . . I can't believe what I did. How I acted. What I put you all through. Please forgive me. Boys, can you forgive me?" Chris, Tommy, and Eli surrounded their dad and hugged him. Popcorn let out a joyful chatter, waving his tail. Charlie gave him an appreciative pat on the head.

Tommy finally broke the huddle. "Sam, you need to get to the cave."

Charlie agreed. "Go, young lady. Hurry. Ash needs you just as much as we all needed him. Go! And when you get there, tell him thank you for me."

A big smile crossed Sam's face. It took a near-tragedy, but they had gotten through to Charlie. The boys had their dad back. Jack had his best friend back, although it would take time for him to get past the pain Charlie had inflicted over the past few days. Despite the hurt Sam endured, she was singularly focused.

"Let's go!" Sam shouted in giddy excitement.

"Go!" replied Tommy. "We'll stay here with Dad. Hurry!"

Sam blew Tommy a kiss, which he pretended to reach out and catch. She and Jack grabbed their packs and hit the trail. The sun was rising with every passing minute as the stars began to fade. They didn't have much time. Ash was waiting.

CHAPTER EIGHTEEN

Jack and Sam had returned to the cliff edge. The sky was glowing to the east beyond the canyon, but the sun had yet to crest the horizon. "We need to hurry, Dad. The sun is almost up." Looking to the cave, they could see Ash's light shining behind the waterfall.

They started down the switchback trail, when Sam heard the familiar voice in her head. *Thank you for saving me, Sam. Thank you for ensuring that my legacy will continue for another thousand years. I will remember you fondly and tell future generations stories of your heroism, your bravery, and your compassion.*

A hauntingly beautiful melody suddenly filled the canyon. Though the song was new to her, Sam recognized Ash's swansong. "No!" Sam yelled, her voice booming an echo through the canyon, nearly overtaking the sound projecting from the cave. "Wait! We're almost . . ." Her plea was cut short, as a pyrotechnic explosion of light blasted from the cave, pushing the waterfall aside and bathing the entire

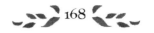

canyon in its warmth. "No!" she yelled again. "Stop! Please!" They were too late. Sam dropped to her knees, sobbing into her hands.

Jack placed a comforting hand on his daughter's shoulder. "I'm so sorry, Princess. I'm sure he waited as long as he could." She offered only a tearful response. Sam knew she would lose him, but all she wanted was to say thank you. It would have been no less difficult in the end. She raised her head from her hands, attempting to wipe her face dry, but the streams continued down her cheeks as she watched the aftermath of Ash's death in the canyon below. The fresh morning air settled back in, and the waterfall resumed its usual course, smoke billowing out of the cave from behind.

Although she had just lost Ash, Sam knew this wasn't the end. If the myth were true, there would be something waiting for them in the burned-out remains of the nest. *The worm!* Sam stood up and brushed herself off, continuing to wipe her eyes and nose, attempting to regain her composure. "Let's go. I need to see." Jack didn't argue. He followed her to the bottom of the canyon.

As they approached the waterfall, the scent of the burning nest filled their noses—sweet and spicy, pungent and sour, off-putting yet intoxicating. "Sam, look," Jack said, motioning to the right side of the waterfall. On the rock was a radiant heart-shaped divot, just like the one from the boulder. Sam looked at her dad and smiled. "Go ahead, Princess, touch it."

Sam moved toward the heart and could feel the heat on

her fingers as she stretched out her arm. She never hesitated. Slowly, she began to trace the heart under her left index finger. The winds remained calm. She looked back at Jack and he nodded, wanting her to continue. Sam closed her eyes in concentration and continued to follow the outline of the heart. The magic of the idol emerged as the falling water slowed. She opened her eyes and continued watching as the waterfall stopped flowing over the cliff altogether! Only residual drops fell from the rock, dripping like an old, leaky faucet. Slowly, Sam removed her finger from the rock; the waterfall remained dry.

Astonished by what they were seeing, Jack and Sam knew something special was waiting for them in the cave. With the waterfall in suspension, the smoke in the cave dissipated quickly and the morning light guided them inside.

As they entered the cavern, they saw it. In the center of the charred nest, partially covered in ash, a little creature squirmed. "The worm," Sam said quietly to herself. Three inches long and mostly green, suggestive of a caterpillar, but not fuzzy. *Feathers?* The little worm had the tiniest of feathers covering its body. As it moved, the colors changed ever so slightly; purples, reds, and oranges glistened along its edges.

Sam reached down and placed the back of her hand in the ash, offering an open palm. "Be careful," her dad warned. She nodded. Slowly the little fellow inched his way into her hand.

"Hi there, little guy." She raised her hand close to her face. Two small but unexpectedly expressive black eyes were

looking back at her. They blinked as if to return her greeting. "I suppose we should call you Ash, too, huh?" The worm glided to Sam's thumb and wrapped itself around, hugging her gently.

"I suppose you have a new friend to take care of for the next three days," Jack said with a chuckle.

Sam laughed, "I guess so. He's so cute." Baby Ash looked up at her, still wrapped around her finger, and blinked a few times. "So I guess you can understand me. Can you talk?" Baby Ash stretched his body skyward and made a sound far more prominent than his tiny stature, reminiscent of a newborn lion cub attempting to roar. Sam giggled at the adorable sound. Ash coiled up, his feathers turning red, as if embarrassed by his emanation. Sam was reassuring. "Soon enough, I suppose." She pet his feathery head. Baby Ash's colors quickly returned as he wrapped himself back around her thumb. Sam turned to her dad. "Back to camp?"

"You betcha, Princess."

As they exited the mouth of the cave, the waterfall resumed flowing at full force with a blast of fine mist rising from the canyon floor. Sam looked back at the heart and watched it slowly fade away as if it had never been there. "Dad . . . the heart. It's gone." Sam ran her fingers over the spot, but the water continued to flow. Her heart sank at the realization. *The vortex is gone. I don't feel dizzy,* she thought, touching her head with her free hand. "We have to get home . . . to Sedona," she said, panicked. "Ash needs the power of a vortex to finish his transformation. It must have used all the power from this place for him to burn. We need to go to Bell Rock. I know there's enough energy there. I feel it every time we drive by. We only have three days to get there."

Jack did his best to keep her calm. "Sam, we will get there. Let's get back to camp, pack up, and get on the road. It's only a couple hours' drive, at best. We have plenty of time." Sam nodded; however, she was still worried. The thought of coming this far and Ash not being able to complete his rebirth frightened her.

When they returned, everyone was excited to see and meet Baby Ash. Even Charlie, who, in his newfound spirit, asked to hold him. It was as if he was a different person altogether from the man who'd been terrorizing them for days. Sam hesitated, but the little worm let Sam know it was okay. "Wow, will you look at that. He's soft," Charlie said, amazed as he stroked a gentle finger down Ash's back, who responded with a repetitive, vibrating twitch. "Do you see that? It's like he's purring." Everyone was thrilled to see Charlie back to himself and laughed at his observation.

Not wanting to lose any more time, Sam reminded the group that they had less than three days before the completion of Ash's metamorphosis. "We need to get everything packed up. We can probably make it back to Sedona by evening." She turned her attention back to Baby

Ash. "As for you, how about a nice, dark, comfy place to rest. You must be tired." The little noodle let out what sounded like a yawn, coiled up, and closed his eyes. Sam wrapped him gently in a soft t-shirt, which she promptly slipped into her backpack.

Everyone scattered through the camp to clean up in preparation for a return to civilization, but it didn't take long before their progress screeched to a halt. "Jack?" Charlie interrupted. "We may have a slight problem." Sam perked up, already annoyed at whatever she was about to hear.

"What kind of problem, Charlie?" questioned Jack.

"In my . . . let's call it 'other state of mind' . . . well . . ."

"Spit it out, Chuck. What's going on?"

Charlie hung his head, not wanting to look anyone in the eyes as he delivered his news. "I may have sliced the distributor wires on your Bronco."

"What?!" Sam yelled in disbelief.

"I had seen what you did to my tires, and I was so mad. I reacted. I'm sorry." Charlie was remorseful, but it didn't subdue Sam's anger.

"How could you?"

Jack intervened. "Compose yourself, Princess. He did that before. When he wasn't himself."

"How are we supposed to get back home? Hitchhike? We're never gonna make it in time!" Sam was dumbfounded and incapable of calming down so they could assess their options.

Tommy chimed in to try and ease her stress. "We'll find

a way, Sam. I know it. Look how far we've come in just a few days. How much we've overcome." Tommy attempted to hug her in hopes it would help, but she briskly shrugged him off.

Once again, Jack attempted to cool her off. Sternly, he responded. "Sam! Charlie made a mistake, and he's sorry about it. That was not the man I've known for more than twenty years. There's nothing we can do about it now. We need to focus on solutions and getting Ash home."

The infuriated look on Sam's face remained, but she relented to her dad's logic. "Fine. What are we supposed to do?"

"Dad's truck still runs, right? Can't we just use the tires from Jack's truck?" Chris offered, not realizing it wasn't as simple as just swapping between the two vehicles.

"Great thought, Chris," said Jack, "but the Bronco uses a different wheel than your dad's truck. Same with the wires—they're not compatible."

They milled around camp in deep thought for a solution, but they were coming up empty until an idea finally sparked for Sam. "Dad, where's the map? I think I have a plan."

Jack rifled through his sack and pulled out the wrinkled, partially torn piece of paper and handed it to Sam. "What are you looking for?"

Sam grabbed the map and flipped it back and forth until she gained her bearings. She traced her finger along the path that led to the cave, then proceeded to move north along

the river until she found what she expected to see. "There! Look. We can follow the river. It might take a day, but it will empty into this reservoir here." She pointed to a large body of water that looked suspiciously like a giant bird. "There's a town near there, and we can get help. We can get the truck fixed so we can get home!"

"Can I see that map?" Charlie asked. He studied Sam's proposed route for a minute. "Jack, you've got yourself one smart cookie here. The river appears to widen about three miles downstream. I have an inflatable raft you guys can take. Perhaps you can make it a bit quicker."

"You're not coming?"

"There's only room for three. I think its best that I stay here and wait for help. I'm still not feeling great anyway." Charlie rubbed the back of his neck. "The boys can stay behind and help me finish packing up while we wait for your return."

"Can I go with them, Dad?" Tommy requested. He'd gone through so much with Sam; he wanted to be there with her to see this through.

Charlie looked to Jack, who nodded his approval. "I guess that's that. Kids, get packed; we need to make sure we're prepared for the long haul. Grab food, a med kit, some tools, and a change of clothes. Something tells me we're not gonna stay dry. We'll leave at first light."

"Daaad," Sam whined. "We still have half a day of light; we should leave as soon as possible! We're already running out of time. According to the map, it should be less than ten miles."

"Yes, but if we don't properly prepare for this and make sure we're rested, we'll never make it in time. We may have a handy map that tells us how to get out of here, but we don't know what we're really up against. Slow and steady, Sam. We'll make it. I promise."

Sam huffed, knowing she wasn't going to get her way. "Fine, but I want to leave by 5 AM," she demanded.

"Yes, ma'am. You have my word. 5 AM sharp," Jack replied, coming to attention like a soldier getting his marching orders.

"Make that 4 AM," she corrected, pushing for more time.

"4:30, and no earlier." Jack put his foot down. Sam smirked at him, proud of her negotiating skills.

They used the rest of the day to ensure they had all the gear they needed for the trek. They studied the map carefully to confirm their route, even noting significant landmarks so they could track their progress and keep themselves on pace.

Once everybody agreed they were adequately prepared, they took the rest of the evening to relax, sit around the fire, and enjoy each other's company for the first time the entire trip. Baby Ash took up residence in Sam's hair, wrapping himself around her braided ponytail lying across the front of her shoulder. Tommy took the opportunity to sit next to them, even putting his arm around her at one point when a cold wind blew through camp. Sam allowed it.

Eli and Popcorn each had a mouth full of food, as usual,

and Chris was giving them grief about it; brotherly love at its finest. Tension remained between Jack and Charlie, but it was subsiding. Charlie seemed back to his old self for the most part, but it was difficult for Jack to forget the awful memories of the last few days. Charlie's behavior had been so bizarre, so out of character, but he was glad to have that episode behind them.

As the evening wore on, the two fathers and old friends reminisced about past trips and discussed plans for their next adventure. The morning would come fast, and they made sure to relish the moment, knowing the impending trek would be challenging.

CHAPTER NINETEEN

4:30 AM came earlier than they expected. Everyone was up to wish Jack, Sam, and Tommy good luck and a speedy return. They had two days to deliver Baby Ash safely to Bell Rock so he could complete his transformation and return to Paradise. They were unsure of the consequences if they failed. Would he remain in worm form? Would he be stuck in the mortal realm for good, becoming mortal himself? Pondering these questions, though, would only distract them from their goal.

Sam, as usual, took command knowing time was of the essence. "Let's hit the road!" She peered into the top of her knapsack to check on Ash. "You ready, little guy?" Ash let out another baby lion roar. He was ready.

"Safe travels, friends," Charlie calmly sent them off, and with that, they started eastward toward the canyon.

At the bottom of the canyon trail, Sam stopped to absorb the beauty of the waterfall and reflect on all they had endured. She hoped that the heart in the rock had returned overnight, but instead, she was met with disappointment. Without any more hesitation, the group made their way down the river. The water moved swiftly, but was far too shallow and rocky to consider using the raft. They would have to stay on foot for now, slowing their progress and adding to Sam's anxiety that they would run out of time.

Jack could read the worry in his daughter's face. "Slow and steady, Sam. We'll get there."

Sam let out a frustrated huff. "Right, slow and steady." She was unhappy with their pace, but knew there wasn't much they could do about it. Hoping to ease her troubles, Sam pulled out the map to study the route more closely. *Two more miles*, she thought, seeing where the river would widen and give them a chance to speed things up. *Two more miles*, she repeated to herself. But before she could finish her thought, a drop fell, hitting her squarely on the forehead. Then another. By the time she looked up, the sky had opened and a deluge came down and pounded them mercilessly. They were without cover; nothing but rocks and small bushes lined the canyon.

"What are we gonna do?" yelled Tommy over the sound of the beating rain echoing through the ravine.

"I have an idea. Tommy, give me a hand," Jack said. He slung his oversized pack off his shoulders and began to untie the giant yellow plastic roll sitting on top. They unfolded the raft and pulled it over their heads and hugged the limestone wall, attempting to fend off the storm. "This should do for now," Jack said proudly of his innovative idea.

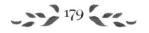

"We're losing time, Dad," Sam whined loudly.

"I think it's best to wait this out. At least until it eases up a bit."

They sat in place, waiting. With each passing minute, Sam grew more agitated. After twenty minutes, the torrent of rain showed no signs of letting up. Before they realized what was happening, the river waters had risen, squeezing them against the canyon wall.

"Dad, this isn't good," Sam said, panicked.

"There's only one thing to do. We need to inflate the raft," Jack replied.

"That'll take forever. The river is rising too fast." Sam looked down to find her shoes almost entirely immersed in the rushing water.

"Just the outer ring. Tommy, you get one side and I'll get the other. If you get tired, switch with Sam. Hurry!"

The water was rising fast. Sam and Tommy switched off every minute, pushing as much air as their lungs could muster into the little tubes. Before they knew it, the water was up to their ankles and the rapids intensified, making it nearly impossible for them to keep their balance. "Hurry, we've almost got it!" Sam shouted at Tommy.

Jack finished his side and relieved Tommy. Completely winded, Tommy dropped his hands to his knees to catch his breath, but immediately lost his footing and fell into the river, away from the shelter of the raft. "TOMMY!" Sam yelled in fright.

Without thought, Jack reacted, dropping the boat from

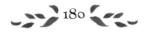

his grip and reaching down to grab Tommy before being washed downstream. The half-inflated raft caught a gust and blew out of their grasp, coming to rest against a large boulder nearly a hundred yards away. The wind and rain continued to batter the raft, which appeared moments from breaking loose and drifting out of sight.

Jack pulled Tommy to his feet, the water now up to their calves. "We need to get to the raft, now!" Jack demanded. "Grab my hand, Princess. Tommy, take Sam's hand and do not let go! Follow me and watch your step." They locked hands and formed a chain. Jack slowly pushed forward through the cold water, leading the way toward the raft, every wading step becoming more dangerous.

Fifty yards.

Twenty-five yards.

Almost there, thought Jack. The once calm, meandering stream was now a raging force stretching across the entire width of the canyon and knee-deep to Jack. Again, Tommy lost his balance and the flood pulled him past Sam, but not from her grip. Sam held on tight, fighting the pull of the water. Jack clutched Sam tightly, but the weight of the kids and slippery footing were too much, plunging them all into the river.

Within seconds, they found themselves pinned to the same rock as the raft. Still hand in hand and clinging to the boulder, Jack was unable to use his free hand to liberate the yellow boat. He had a choice to make. Knowing their only hope was to ride out the riptides inside the raft, he started to loosen his grip on Sam and Tommy, but he couldn't bring himself to fully commit.

Sam could hear her dad's inner struggle. "It's alright, Dad. Let us go, we'll be okay." Jack hesitated, but Sam helped him by releasing her hand from his. The kids screamed as they washed downstream, still holding on to each other, their heads bobbing up and down, barely clear of the surface.

With the kids drifting away, Jack pulled and tugged on the raft until he freed it from the boulder. He pulled himself across the outer ring of the inner tube and into the center of the deflated boat. He made his way down the river, fighting the rapids and boulders, which pushed on the bottom of the raft, making it difficult to hold on. He was tossed like a ragdoll, but managed to reach over his shoulder and pull a collapsible plastic oar from its hold. Within seconds, Jack had caught up to the kids.

Using the paddle as a lifeline, Jack shouted over the roaring rapids. "Grab on!"

Sam and Tommy continued to scream for help, flailing for the outstretched oar. Every time they got close, the river sent them in the opposite direction. Looking ahead, Jack could see a series of massive boulders creating a giant wave and funneling through a narrow gap to the other side. He knew if he didn't get to the kids, they could be smashed against the rocks, but it was approaching fast . . . too fast to get there in time.

"Kids!" he yelled to get their attention. "Rocks! Hold your breath and duck!" he demanded at full volume. Sam

turned her head just in time to see the fast-approaching boulders and giant waves. She and Tommy inhaled as deep as they could, still gripping each other tight, and submerged from Jack's view. The tiny, half-inflated craft rocked from side to side, shooting through a flume between two giant boulders and safely to the other side. As he emerged, the waters became noticeably calmer, and without any further rapids in view, he began looking for the kids.

"Dad! Dad!" Sam yelled, drowning out Tommy's own pleas for help in the process.

Jack used the oar to row himself toward the kids and pull them into the boat. "Are you okay?" he asked. In his worry, he didn't give them a chance to answer, "Are you hurt? I'm sorry, I didn't know what else to do. We needed the raft, and I didn't realize it was going to get that bad." He was begging for forgiveness, unaware that Sam had made the decision to let go for him.

"It's okay, Dad," Sam chimed in. "You had to do what you had to do. It was the right thing." She looked over at Tommy, "Are you okay?"

"Fine, just cold," Tommy replied. He was thankful to be alive, but was no longer worried about himself. "Baby Ash!" he exclaimed.

Sam pulled the water-logged bag off her back and carefully loosened the drawstring. She reached in and pulled out the shirt containing Ash. "Oh, no. No, no, no," she repeated. As she swiftly unraveled the wet ball of material, something strange appeared in place of the little worm. *A cocoon!* "Whoa!" Jack and Tommy leaned in for a closer look, forgetting that the raft wasn't sufficiently stable and throwing them all off balance. Sam managed to keep hold of the shirt and the cocoon, shooting them a disapproving glare in the process. "Careful, please!" she scolded.

Jack and Tommy carefully drew near for a better glimpse. "Is he alive?" Tommy asked.

"I'm not . . ." Sam was cut off by the wriggling of the now encased worm. "Apparently so," she said with a relieved smile. Sam continued to examine the covering. It was soft and silky, like the ones she had seen so many times while chasing butterflies. She looked up to her dad. "He must be getting ready."

Jack nodded in agreement. "If it wasn't for that shell, the little guy might not have made it. We owe it to him more than ever to make sure he gets home safely and finishes his transformation."

The rain continued to fall, though more lightly, as they made their way down the now lazy river. Jack pulled the second oar from his pack and handed it to Tommy. They carefully paddled downstream, maneuvering the raft around the boulders and tree branches that sprung from the water. Sam continued to hold Baby Ash, now under cover of her jacket, in hopes he'd dry out. She wasn't sure it was even necessary, but wanted to keep him safe, nonetheless.

The sun finally popped back out after an uneventful hour on the water. Jack was able to finish inflating the raft while Tommy captained the ship. Sam allowed the warm rays of the sun to reach the cocoon, as she pet it with a soft finger. Ash seemed to enjoy it, as the wriggling picked up.

"Tommy, can you?" She held out Ash and transferred him to Tommy, who held his hands together like he was scooping water from the river. He knew how precious the cargo was and wanted to be cautious.

Sam pulled out the map and gently unfolded it, trying to avoid tearing the damp paper. "We should be hitting the reservoir soon. Less than a mile," she proclaimed.

"Perfect," Jack responded. "Once we get there, keep an eye out. Hopefully, someone will be nearby and able to help us."

Sam returned the map to her backpack and resumed her watchful sentry over Ash. Tommy and Jack, determined to make up time, paddled hard to pick up speed. Within twenty minutes, the little yellow craft emerged from the canyon and spilled into an enormous body of water. They surveyed the surroundings, searching for some semblance of life near the shore. It wouldn't take long.

"There!" Tommy shouted, pointing to a cabin just west of their position.

"Paddle," Jack demanded. Tommy and Jack put their oars in the water and propelled the boat as fast as they could. Young Ponderosas lined the lakeshore beach and surrounded the old wooden building. The back end of a Jeep peeked out from behind the structure. "Help!" Sam shouted, over and over. "We need help." But no one responded. Tommy joined Sam's calls for help, but their pleas went unreturned. There were no signs of life as they drifted ashore.

Jack jumped out and pulled the raft halfway out of the water, allowing the kids to disembark safely and remain dry. Tommy briefly continued calling for help until interrupted by Sam. "There's no one here."

"It doesn't appear so, Princess. Maybe we should go knock, just to be sure," Jack suggested.

Sam proceeded toward the front of the cabin, rapping on the door as loud as she could. "Hello? Is anybody home?" Still, no answer.

"I guess not," Tommy rhetorically interjected. Sam rolled her eyes.

"Maybe we should wait. They can't be far, there's a Jeep parked in back," said Jack.

"We can't keep waiting, Dad. I know, I know . . . slow and steady. But we're running out of time."

They walked around the perimeter of the cabin, looking for signs of life. Jack approached the car and placed a hand on the hood, but it was cold; no sign of recent use. Sam approached the back door of the cabin and immediately noticed it was ajar. She knocked loudly and shouted into the house, "Hello? Hello? Anyone there?" As expected, there was no answer, but the door creaked open at the force of her hand. Sam looked at her dad for permission to enter. He shook his head in disapproval, but Sam just shrugged her shoulders

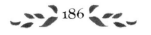

and continued inside, unabated.

"Sam, no! Get back here. You can't just walk into someone else's home." But Jack's words fell on deaf ears as he chased behind to try and keep her out of trouble. Tommy followed, not wanting to miss out.

Once inside, the cabin décor grabbed their attention; it felt as though they'd stepped back into the 1970s—green shag carpeting, wood-paneled walls covered in taxidermy, plaid drapes that only allowed small streams of light through the grime-covered windows. It was eerie, and Tommy decided it best to wait outside. He'd seen his share of horror movies—without Charlie's knowledge, of course—and more often than not, there was a creepy empty house involved.

Jack continued to pursue his daughter, who swiftly made it to the far side of the house and into the lone bedroom. "Sam, get out of here now. This isn't our house. We're trespassing."

"Dad, come here! Check this out." As Jack entered the bedroom, he noticed the same dusty furnishings as the rest of the house, but what Sam had found quickly drew his gaze. It was an unusually large egg, propped upright on an acrylic ring that held it in place.

"An ostrich egg?" Jack guessed. But he knew that wasn't the case. The egg sparkled, even in the musty darkness of the room. As he got closer, he could see that it was opaque, and suspended inside was a familiar form . . . *A phoenix.* Albeit on a much smaller scale, there was no doubt what they were seeing. "This can't be real. Can it?" he asked, looking to

Sam for an answer.

"I'm not sure, but if it is, we probably shouldn't stick around. Baby Ash is in danger here. We need to go." Sam grabbed the egg and headed out of the cabin. She knew that if it were real, it needed rescuing.

As they ran out of the house, Jack noticed a set of keys hanging next to the door and swiped them. "Get in the Jeep now! Let's go!" Tommy turned, unsure of what was going on or what they had seen, but didn't waste time jumping in the car. Jack slid into the driver seat and turned on the ignition, but the engine refused to cooperate. He tried again and again, but the motor wouldn't turn over.

"Hey, stop! That's my car! What are you doing?" They turned to see a woman in a red and black flannel shirt running toward them, armed with a shotgun in one hand and what looked like a pheasant in the other. "Stop!" she repeated.

Jack turned the keys one more time, and the engine roared to life. He hit the gas and kicked up a cloud of dust and dirt, shielding them from the woman's view. Not willing to slow down, Jack darted through the trees, making his own path away from the woman and through the forest. Once they reached the road, he straightened the wheel and accelerated.

"What's going on?" Tommy popped his head up from the back seat.

"This is what's going on," replied Sam, picking up the egg from her lap to show Tommy.

"Is that Ash?" he asked incredulously.

"No, it's another phoenix, and that woman had it

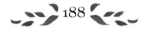

sitting out on display. Not exactly friendly if you ask me," Sam retorted.

"We need to get help for Charlie and the boys," Jack responded. "As soon as we see a place to stop, we need to call a park ranger."

"There's no time, Dad. We just broke into someone's home and stole their car . . . and their phoenix egg. We need to get to Sedona!"

Jack knew his daughter was right. If they stopped now, they risked not making it in time, not to mention getting arrested, which was a likely scenario given that they were driving a stolen car. "Ok, Princess, but as soon as we get home, we're returning the car and apologizing to that lady. Hopefully, she won't press charges."

Sam was content knowing they were on their way to fulfill Ash's fate. She reached into her backpack and pulled out the shirt, to check on him. As she pulled open the fabric, she found another surprise. The cocoon had grown to the size of a chicken egg, and the once soft exterior was beginning to harden. She showed Tommy and Jack, who were both stunned by the quick growth and continued metamorphosis. She held up Ash next to the egg from the cabin. Unlike the larger egg, Ash's was light blue with only hints of a sparkle, and dabbed with small, dark purple splotches. It was clear that Ash's egg would soon be the size of the other, and perhaps even look like it.

"Dad?" Sam said. "Thank you for believing in me. For believing in Ash and helping him. I love you."

"I love you too, sweetheart. I'd do anything for you," Jack replied. Sam smiled big as he placed a hand on her head and messed her hair.

They continued down the bumpy road, passing a big green sign with white lettering: Sedona 120 Miles. In a few short hours, they'd reach their destination and Ash would be one step closer to Paradise. They had less than 36-hours to spare, and any more setbacks would surely make their task impossible. Jack kept the Jeep steady and at the speed limit, pushing toward home.

CHAPTER TWENTY

What should have been a relatively quick drive seemed to stretch on forever. Jack stayed the course, but Sam couldn't sit still. Her frustration and anxiety were growing with every passing mile. "Dad, can you drive faster?"

"I'm going as fast I can, Sam. We'll make it in plenty of time, I promise. We're only about thirty miles out." Suddenly, an orange light illuminated on the dash; the gas tank was dwindling fast. *Great,* he thought with a heavy sigh, which didn't get past Sam's omniscient gaze.

"What? What's wrong?"

"Well . . . seems we're running pretty low on gas. We need to stop, or we'll never make it." Sam didn't say a word. Her sharp glare said it all, and Jack was defenseless. "It'll be quick. Don't worry." She averted her eyes, staring back out toward the mountains rolling past the passenger-side window.

Three miles later, Jack exited the highway. "There!"

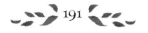

Sam exclaimed, pointing to the gas station at the top of the off-ramp.

"I see it. We'll be in and out in no time."

Jack raced to the top of the exit, ready to pull in, but they never expected what awaited them. At the gas station, two Arizona patrol cars sat parked, fronting the attached convenience store. As they came to a stop at the top of the ramp, they looked at each other, not convinced what the correct move was.

"Great, now what?" Tommy asked.

"Dad?" Sam followed.

Jack sat and thought for a brief second before pulling the car forward across the intersection and into the gas station. "Just act normal." He brought the old Jeep to a stop at the furthest pump from the storefront, the squeal and screech from the brakes letting everyone know they'd arrived. Heads of annoyed patrons turned in their direction as two uniformed officers pushed through the doors of the store, unaware of the ruckus they just missed. Jack, Sam, and Tommy sat motionless, watching as the officers made their way to their vehicles, slushies in hand, oblivious, joking and laughing.

"Well?" Sam asked.

"Here, take this and go inside. Grab some snacks and tell them you want $20 in gas." Jack handed Sam several bills. "Don't draw attention to yourselves; just act normal. Tommy, go with Sam. Low profile," he whispered.

Sam snatched the cash from Jack's hand and opened

the car door, which immediately greeted them with a rusty squeak. Sam instinctively pulled the door toward her a bit to stop the sound. The two officers took notice, glancing in their direction. Sam ducked her head below the Jeep's dashboard to avoid being seen. She waited briefly before popping her head back up to see that the policemen had returned to their conversation, not giving them a second thought. Slowly, Sam continued to open the door, cautious this time to keep any extraneous creaks and groans to a minimum. Tommy hopped out behind her and shut the door, but not as inconspicuously as Sam would have preferred. The rusty hinges once again wailed as the door slammed. Tommy gave Sam an apologetic look.

Jack remained in the car, waiting for them to return so he could pump the gas. As Sam and Tommy passed the patrolmen he watched for any reactions, but saw nothing. *Phew,* he thought. The two men remained propped against their respective cars, talking. *Go already!* Jack was growing more and more nervous waiting for them to leave, preferably before the kids walked back out.

Sam and Tommy stuck to each other's sides as they weaved their way through the tiny store. Their attempt to look normal was in vain, as they nervously shuffled from aisle to aisle, grabbing bags of chips, candy, and beef jerky. "Let's get something to drink and get out of here," Sam suggested.

They made their way to the counter and plopped down their load of goodies. The cashier was an older, personable woman, eager to talk to her customers and make them feel welcome. "Howdy, kiddos. How are you doing this fine day?"

"Doing fine, ma'am," Tommy responded shyly.

"It sure is a nice day out there. Where y'all headed today? Anywhere fun?"

"Just home," Sam responded shortly, not wanting to drag out the exchange. The cashier continued to ring up their items, taking the hint that the kids weren't much for conversation, or perhaps just wary of strangers. "Oh, and $20 of gas, please," Sam finished.

"Sure thing, sweetheart. Which vehicle is yours?"

"It's the . . ." Sam stopped midsentence as she looked up toward the Jeep and noticed that her dad was no longer in the car. Her attention was quickly pulled away by a commotion just outside the doors to the mart, near the police cars. Through the windowed double doors, she could see her dad's head being pushed down by one of the officers, clearing his way into the back of their vehicle.

"Never a dull moment around here," the cashier quipped.

Not wanting to draw any attention, Sam calmly engaged the lady behind the counter. "I guess not," she replied with a nervous chuckle. Sam elbowed Tommy to grab their sundries, as she smiled and handed the lady the money.

"You still need gas, sweetheart?" she asked. Sam had hoped that in the excitement of the activity outside, she'd have forgotten and they could make their escape.

"Uh . . . oh yeah, yeah. I forgot." Sam, wary of pointing

out the Jeep, glanced again through the store window, thankful for the big red numbers emblazoned above the pumps. "Number 13, please."

The cashier pushed a few buttons on the screen in front of her, handed over the change, and bid them farewell. "Have a good day now . . . and stay out of trouble." Sam wasn't happy with the added comment, but she was pretty sure the lady didn't realize that the person being hauled off belonged with them.

Sam turned to Tommy with a whisper. "Head down, follow me. Not a word." Tommy nodded in compliance.

Upon exiting, Sam turned away from the police cars, spying her dad out of the corner of her eye. She continued around the edge of the building and out of sight from the officers, Tommy in tow.

"What are we supposed to do now?" Tommy asked.

Sam glanced around the corner to see what was going on. The officers were in their vehicles with the lights flashing. Jack sat in the back seat of the nearest cruiser with his head dropped in shame, not wanting to be seen. Slowly, both cars began to back out of their parking spots. As the car with her dad stopped, he pulled his head up and made eye contact with Sam. "I'm sorry. I love you," he mouthed. A quick burst of the police siren rang out as they pulled out of the gas station. Sam ducked back behind the building and slid down the wall to the ground, defeated and desperate.

"We need to get outta here," Tommy said. "I'll drive."

"You know how to drive?" Sam asked in disbelief.

"Well, I've never actually driven, but it doesn't seem too hard." Sam raised an eyebrow, still not convinced of Tommy's acumen behind the wheel. He quickly defended his decision. "I've been in the car when my dad was teaching Chris. I can do it."

Sam knew they didn't have another choice. "Ok then, gas it up and let's go." A look of confusion crossed Tommy's face. "What's the matter?"

"I . . . I've never put gas in a vehicle. I'm not exactly sure how to pump the gas."

"Really, Tommy? Ugh. I'll figure it out. Just get in."

Sam and Tommy stealthily made their way to the Jeep. Sam fumbled with the nozzle for a few minutes before finally engaging the latch and starting the flow of gas. She stood there, arms crossed, in a glow of pride at being able to figure it out on her own. In her satisfaction, she failed to notice the police car pulling into the gas station parking lot and into the same spot as the car which had just hauled away her dad.

"Sam! Sam!" Tommy yelled in a whisper. Sam was pulled from her moment of pleasure as Tommy's words snapped her to attention. "Get in," he continued, pointing to the squad car. Sam slipped into the Jeep just as the gas pump handle clicked, indicating it was finished.

Keeping a low profile, they watched as a woman emerged from the passenger door of the patrol car. She was in her early forties, with dark brown eyes and long, tawny brown hair, which she wore in a tight bun. Sam recognized the plaid flannel shirt; it was the same lady they had left in a cloud of dust at the cabin, undoubtedly brought back by the police to retrieve her car.

"Get in the back," Sam demanded. They scurried behind the seats and under an old wool blanket the woman kept in the Jeep. "Stay down and be quiet."

Outside, the voices of the woman and the police officer could be overheard. Sam and Tommy stayed still and quietly waited in their hiding spot, not sure if they'd get caught or if they'd be driven back to the reservoir. Neither sounded appealing, and time was running out.

As the voices drew closer, Sam realized her backpack was still on the ground in the front seat, tucked against the underside of the dashboard. "Ash," she whispered to Tommy, panicked. "I need to get him." Tommy shook his head no, sure that any movement would give away their position, but Sam decided it was worth the risk. She started to pull the itchy grey covers off of her head, but the driver's door began to creak open. Sam dipped back under the blanket.

"Well looks like you at least got some gas out of this," said the officer as the woman jumped behind the wheel. "Does it look like anything is missing?" The kids' eyes locked in fear that she'd see the backpack.

The woman glanced around the vehicle. "No, sir. I don't think they took anything. I hope you're able to find those poor kids, for their sake. I'm sure they're scared. Please let me know if I need to come to the station and make a statement."

"Yes, ma'am. Drive safe, and we'll be in touch." The

door slammed shut, and the loud engine came to life. Sam and Tommy were terrified, not sure how they'd get out of this predicament. Worse than getting caught, though, Sam was more concerned they would not get Ash to Bell Rock safely in time.

The woman pulled out of the station and made several turns before accelerating to what felt like highway speeds. Sam and Tommy remained hidden under the blanket, unsure which direction they were headed. After twenty minutes of driving, the old jalopy pulled to the side of the road and came to an eerily quiet stop. No high pitched brake noises and even the idle from the engine appeared to keep to a low timbre. The kids could hear the woman rustling in the front seat, and it didn't take long for Sam to realize she had discovered the backpack. She started breathing heavily, and Tommy was fearful she would hyperventilate under the hot confines of the blanket. The concern was short-lived as they were flooded by light and fresh air, the woman ripping off their covering, exposing them to the incoming sun.

"Hello there, rascals," the woman said plainly. The kids didn't respond, frozen in fear. The woman waited for a response, but almost immediately realized she wasn't going to get one. "You have no idea what kind of trouble you're in."

Sam attempted to speak up. "Please . . . we're sorry. We were . . ."

"We were what?" the lady interrupted. "Stealing my most beloved possession?" She grabbed the giant opaque phoenix egg from the front passenger seat, placing it in view of the kids. "Do you even know what this is? Or did you just think this was some bauble collecting dust on my nightstand?" The woman was upset, but maintained her composure, keeping an even but stern tone. Nevertheless, she seemed menacing to Sam and Tommy, who were understandably frightened.

"Ma'am," Tommy shyly spoke up. "We're really sorry."

"Sorry for what? Breaking into my cabin? Stealing my egg? Stealing old Betty here?" she asked, slapping her hand solidly on the steering wheel.

"Yes. We're sorry for all of it," Sam replied softly. "We were just trying to save our friend, and when we found the cabin, we were looking for help."

Sam was hesitant to offer up any more information, but the woman insisted. "Go on." Sam and Tommy pulled themselves up from their hiding spot and onto the back seat.

"We shouldn't have gone into your house. The door was open, and we were hoping someone was inside. We got scared and took your car because we needed to get back to Sedona. We swear, we were going to return it immediately," Sam pleaded.

The woman sat silently, contemplating. "Tell me more about this friend of yours you were trying to save. Where is he? Is he the one that helped you steal my car?"

"No," Sam replied. "That's my dad. We were trying to save Tommy's dad and brothers. They're stuck at a campsite upriver from the reservoir."

"You're Tommy?" Tommy nodded. "So if you're trying

to save your *friends*," she continued, placing heavy emphasis on the plurality of the word, "then please explain to me why you're driving back to Sedona? And why did you leave me in a trail of dust if you were looking for help?"

"We got scared. We saw your gun, and we thought you were gonna shoot at us."

The woman started to laugh heartily. "Shoot you?" What kind of monster do you think I am, darlin'?" She continued to laugh.

Sam interrupted the woman's moment of hilarity. "After we saw the egg, we thought . . . and then the gun. We freaked out and ran."

"The egg scared you?" "And why is that? There'd be no reason to be scared unless you know something about this egg. So enlighten me."

Sam paused, knowing her response would open a bag of worms, but she decided the truth was best. "It's a phoenix egg. It's special."

"That it is, Miss . . ." the woman paused, waiting for her reply.

"Sam. My name is Sam Owsian."

"So, Miss Sam Owsian . . . you appear to be a pretty smart young lady. Tell me more about this egg." Sam paused. "It's ok, you can tell me. I just want to hear you say it."

"This phoenix didn't get to be reborn. It's trapped in the egg forever. And you had it sitting there like a decoration." Sam tried her best to remain even-keeled but couldn't help getting in a dig.

"Dear Sam, this is anything but a decoration to me. This here is my life's greatest regret," she continued, holding up the egg and allowing the sunlight to penetrate the shell, the phoenix inside suspended in a shower of glittering light. "The last thing this is, is a decoration. Because of me, this little guy didn't get to return to Paradise."

"Wait, you . . . you know about Paradise? That was your phoenix?" Sam was in disbelief.

"Sam, Tommy . . . meet Cinder. And you can call me Mick." She handed the egg to Sam. "I found Cinder just north of Sedona on a hike just about nine years ago. I had heard of phoenixes, but didn't know much about them. She could talk to me with her mind. Turns out, I could talk to her, too. She told me that to be reborn and return home, she'd need the power of a vortex. I've lived in Sedona most of my life, so I immediately knew where to take her."

"Bell Rock," Sam interjected.

"Yes, that's right. How did you know that?"

Sam handed the egg to Tommy and lunged over the front seat, tentatively grabbing her backpack. She reached inside, but hesitated and looked to Tommy for permission. He nodded. "She can help us," Tommy said.

Sam pulled the tee-shirt from her sack and began to unwrap its contents. Even Sam was surprised by the reveal. Ash's cocoon had more than doubled in size, and the soft exterior had almost fully hardened into a shell . "Mick, meet Ash. He's the reason for all of this. We need to get him to Bell Rock so he can finish his transformation."

"Magnificent," Mick said in amazement, reaching out to hold the egg. "I think we better get this little guy to his destination then."

"But what about my dad? And Chris and Eli? Your dad?" Tommy asked.

Mick settled his concerns, "Don't worry; I'll make some phone calls. I'll have someone up to get your family before dusk. As for your dad, I'll call the station and tell them I'm not pressing charges. That it was all a big misunderstanding." Sam couldn't believe her luck. So much had gone wrong, and yet here they were closing in on their destiny . . . on Ash's destiny.

Mick finished making the calls, then fired the Jeep back up and kept driving; they were only ten miles from Sedona. Charlie, Chris, and Eli would be picked up by a park ranger and taken to Mick's cabin, where they could rest and recuperate. Jack would be released within the hour and escorted to Sedona, to be reunited with his daughter and Tommy.

CHAPTER TWENTY-ONE

oon Bell Rock was in view, and the intense energy within the vortex swirled through Sam's head. It was fiercely debilitating, as she grabbed her head and winced. Tommy grabbed her hand to comfort her. Mick, glancing in the rearview mirror, noticed Sam's reaction to the rock. "Are you okay, darlin'?"

Tommy spoke for Sam. "It's the vortex. She's sensitive to it."

"Sam, you have a gift. But I'm guessing you already know that, don't you?"

Sam answered weakly, "Yes, ma'am. Ash told me before he died."

"I have the gift too. It wasn't until Cinder showed up that I figured that out. Before that, I just assumed I was one of the few people around these parts that was affected by the powers of the local rocks. One of the ones that gets the headaches and dizzy spells. It's taken me many years, but I've finally learned to control it. I can help you control your gift

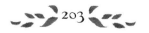

too, and learn how to tap into it and use it for good."

As they continued past Bell Rock, Sam's head started to clear. "Wait, where are we going? Why are we passing the rock?" Sam asked sternly.

"We're heading to my place," Mick answered. "We'll wait for your dad and the others there. Don't worry; Ash can't do his thing until dawn anyway. In the meantime, we can work on those powers of yours. There's a vortex in my backyard. It's not like Bell Rock or some of the others around here, but it's strong enough that you can start practicing."

Sam knew she was right. There was nothing they could do right now, but the thought of not having Ash waiting at the vortex worried her. "Ash told me to find someone who could help me. You'd do that for me?"

"I'd be happy to. I didn't have anyone to guide me. I had to figure it out on my own. Besides, based on your reaction back there, I can tell you're far more gifted than I am." Mick smiled wide and turned her attention back to the road. "We're almost there, just another few minutes. My place is up past the airport."

The airport was another hotspot that Sam wasn't fond of. It wasn't as strong as Bell Rock, but still caused a reaction that made her swoon. As they neared the airport, Sam began to grimace. Tommy put his arm around her and pulled her into his chest. The feeling was fleeting, dissipating almost as fast as it came on.

"Thank you," Sam said to Tommy, with a kiss on the cheek. Mick caught the loving act in the mirror and couldn't

help but grin. *Ah, young love,* she thought, pretending not to notice. Sam blushed, having heard Mick's thought. She'd keep her ability to read minds to herself for now, at least until she was sure she could trust the friendly stranger.

The Jeep slowed and pulled up a small steep hill. The kids jolted from side to side with the bumps in the road. "Welcome to Cinder Ranch," Mick proclaimed, coming to a stop in front of a small adobe style house.

Not much of a ranch, Sam thought. As they exited the car, Sam and Tommy immediately were drawn to the phoenix-shaped symbol painted black on the teal garage door. "Whoa," exclaimed Sam.

"You like that, huh? Painted that myself. After Cinder came along, I guess you could say I became a bit obsessed. The power, magic, and beauty of these birds is something else. Come on inside, I'll show you the rest." Mick waved them into the house.

Sam and Tommy entered the house and stepped into another world. The walls were painted in fiery hues and adorned with mythological imagery from phoenix lore. A large, stuffed phoenix hung from the vaulted ceiling overlooking the living room. Its wings were spread wide, its tail feathers falling to the ground in the far corner of the room. "Is that . . . ?" Tommy asked.

"Oh, dear no, son, I made that myself. Papier mache and lots of glue and fake feathers," Mick responded. "Come, check out the back."

They stepped into what Mick referred to as the

backyard, and found themselves overlooking a small grass lawn, which opened to a five-acre landscape, hugged by red rocks on each side. The far end of the expanse was closed off by another red stone wall that reached thirty feet high, creating a horseshoe-shaped canyon filled with evergreens. An old corral hugged the canyon to the left side of the property. Inside were two chestnut mares who whinnied at the sight of Mick.

"Can we pet them?" Sam asked.

"Be my guest, darlin', mi casa es su casa," she replied.

Sam carefully shed her backpack and offered it to Mick, "Would you mind?"

"Not at all," she said, accepting the precious cargo inside. "Go have fun."

Sam and Tommy raced to the corral and jumped onto the lower rung of the enclosure. The horses met them, eager for attention and perhaps a treat. As they pet the powerful creatures, Tommy broke the silence. "How are you feeling?"

"Nervous . . . but good, I suppose."

"You're not feeling anything? Mick said there was a vortex back here."

"Yeah, you're right. I'm not feeling anything," Sam said, perplexed.

"You don't think she made it up, do you?" Tommy questioned, suspicious of Mick's intentions. They looked back toward the house, but Mick was no longer outside, having returned to the confines of the house with Ash.

"I don't know, but maybe we should get back to the

house. She has Ash, and I don't think we should let him, or her, out of our sights again."

Sam's anxiety flared again, but Tommy had come to recognize the signs; he put a hand on her shoulder. "I'm right by your side, through all of this. I'm here for you and Ash. Whatever you need."

Sam pursed her lips tight in a dimpled smile, "I know. Thank you, Ani."

"Ani?"

"Yeah, like Anikan." Sam turned and started walking back to the house. Tommy quickly put two and two together, remembering how Chris called her padawan. *Wait, is she saying I'm her boyfriend?* Tommy blushed and started walking fast to catch up to Sam. When he did, he boldly grabbed her hand and they continued to the house, fingers interlocked.

As they reached the back door, multiple voices spilled from inside. Jack was standing there, flanked by a sheriff's deputy. "Dad!" Sam yelled, releasing Tommy's hand and running into her father's arms. Jack picked her up and swung her around, ecstatic to see her safe and sound, nearly hitting the deputy in the process. "Are you okay?" she asked as he set her back on her feet.

"Fine, Princess. I'm just thankful Ms. Brown here is so forgiving. And now I know why," he said, motioning to all the phoenix paraphernalia.

"When are my dad and brothers getting here?" Tommy asked.

"They'll be up in the next day or two," responded the

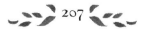

deputy. "We have a ranger with them to make sure they're okay. Once they get the trucks running, they'll be on their way. If you're all okay here, I'll be heading out." The officer tipped his flat-brimmed hat to the group and exited.

Sam turned to see Ash's egg sitting on the coffee table. She ran swiftly and grabbed it, holding it upright, wrapped in both arms. "What are you doing?" Sam asked Mick, annoyed.

"Oh, I'm sorry. I was just checking him out. He's really growing."

Sam sat on the couch and began examining the egg. The light blue exterior remained, but the purple spots had lightened, replaced with shimmering sparkles—the egg was only slightly smaller than Cinder's.

"Wow, it's really changed a lot," Jack observed.

"I think I'll hold on to him until it's time," Sam warned. "Ash has been through enough."

"So . . . where's this vortex in your yard?" Tommy said, changing the subject. He could feel Sam getting frustrated, but wanted to determine if Mick was telling the truth.

"Follow me," Mick commanded happily.

They returned to the backyard, Sam still clutching the egg tight, not giving up control to anyone. Mick led them to the back of the property on a trail that wound through the grove of trees. Dusk was settling in as they reached the far canyon wall. Sam's head began to swirl, and she briefly stumbled. Tommy caught her by the elbow with one hand and cradled the egg with his other, helping Sam maintain her

grip.

"Sam . . . are you okay?" Jack asked.

"Yeah, fine, Dad," she said, shaking her head clear. As she regained her bearings, Sam noticed a small phoenix design on the top of a large tree stump. It was the same design as the garage.

"That's the center point of the vortex. It's very tight, and doesn't extend much past about ten feet. Like I said, it's not as powerful as the others, but it'll be good for you to practice with," offered Mick.

Sam decided there was only one way to start overcoming her sensitivity to the powerful forces. She handed the egg to Tommy, and jumped directly onto the tree stump. As she landed, she immediately dropped to one knee and grabbed her head with both hands. A fierce wind enveloped the area, kicking up leaves and debris. The concern on Jack's and Tommy's faces was apparent; Mick remained stoic, knowing what Sam was experiencing and confident in her ability to overcome and control the vortex.

Sam, still kneeling, placed her hands flat on the stump. She raised her head to the sky, and her eyes glazed over, filling a solid iridescent blue. The swirling leaves were becoming interwoven with swirls of light, which now emanated from Sam's fingertips.

"Sam!" Tommy yelled. The wind stopped as if by command, and the lights faded. Sam fell from the stump and onto the ground. "Sam!" Tommy shouted again, rushing to her side. She laid there unconscious, her hair a mess, and full of leaves.

"Let's get her inside. She needs to rest," said Mick.

Jack picked up his limp daughter and carried her across the property. Tommy followed, holding the egg tightly and refusing to let go.

Once inside, Jack laid Sam on the couch. "I think we should call a doctor;"

"She'll be okay. She has to learn how to let the energy flow through her, to control the power, and not let it control her." Mick was adamant that Sam would be okay, but Jack and Tommy weren't so trusting. "She just needs rest, I promise. Why don't you put her in my room, so she's more comfortable?"

With darkness fully set in, Mick walked through the house lighting candles. Although she had electricity, she wasn't keen on using it, preferring to live off-the-grid as much as possible. The candlelight danced through the living room, creating eerie shadows and a menacing presence from the phoenix above. Tommy sat on the bed next to Sam, holding the egg on his lap, while stroking her hair with his other hand. He hoped she'd be okay as Mick promised, but still didn't trust her intent, despite the vortex being real.

Midnight came and passed. Mick was asleep on the couch while Jack slept on an old, weathered leather recliner. Tommy snored lightly, sleeping upright next to Sam. He maintained

positive control of the egg under a thick crocheted blanket, his free hand intertwined with Sam's.

The distant yips and howls of a pack of coyotes echoed through the canyon and caused Sam to rouse. She opened her eyes slowly, realizing she was in a strange bed, but quickly surmising it must be Mick's. She gently pulled her hand from Tommy's grip and sat up. She grabbed her head, which slightly throbbed.

"Sam, are you okay?" Tommy whispered, startling her.

"Tommy, what happened? My head is killing me. The last thing I remember was jumping onto that tree stump."

"You've been asleep for over 24-hours," he replied. "We thought it was best to just let you sleep and recover." Tommy recounted the episode. Her glowing eyes. The sparks from her fingers. The wind.

"Wait, what time is it?" Sam said, panicked.

Tommy glanced at the clock on the nightstand. "3:30, if that thing's correct."

"We only have a few hours left. We need to get Ash to . . . Ash! Where's Ash?" Sam cried out.

"It's okay, he's right here," said Tommy, uncovering the egg from underneath the blanket. Ash's egg was now every bit the size of Cinder's. It glowed, with opalescent spots. Sam took the egg from Tommy and made her way toward the candle on the dresser. She held it up, and the unmistakable shape of a phoenix emerged. She couldn't look away.

"Did you see that?" Sam asked Tommy.

"It's beautiful," Tommy replied.

"No, look closer." Tommy jumped out of bed to get the best possible view, and stared at the egg. "There!" The little phoenix inside twitched slightly. Then again.

"Incredible," Tommy whispered.

Despite every effort to stay hush, their conversation woke Jack, who poked his head in through the bedroom door. "How are you feeling, Princess?"

"Why did you let me sleep so long? We need to get to Bell Rock now!" Sam proclaimed. Jack checked his watch and saw they were running out of time.

"You needed the rest. Tommy took good care of you and Ash. He refused to leave your side." Jack said.

"Dad, we need to go." Sam was panicked. "We only have a few hours."

"You're right. Get packed. I'll go wake Mick."

As Jack exited, Sam turned to Tommy, "I still don't trust her."

"Me either, but we need her. I don't think she'd be very forgiving if we stole her car again." Sam agreed.

She finished stuffing her backpack, Ash safe and sound inside, and headed for the front door. Mick emerged with Jack, keys in hand, and ready to set out for their destination. Dawn was less than three hours away, and Ash had a birthday to celebrate. Sam was nervous, not just for Ash, but for herself. If the vortex in Mick's canyon was any indication, Bell Rock had something big in store for her.

CHAPTER TWENTY-TWO

S
am leapt from the Jeep before it could come to a complete stop, eager to get Ash to the epicenter of the vortex—perhaps too eager. As her feet hit the ground, she dropped to her knees and grabbed her head in pain. Tommy, as always, was there to catch and steady her. He slowly pulled Sam to her feet.

"Take it easy," Tommy requested. "We have time. Don't overdo it."

"Sorry," Sam replied. "I just want to get there."

Mick chimed in as she exited the driver's seat, "We all do, but you're still a little weak from the backyard vortex. In time you'll learn to control your powers instead of it controlling you."

"Slow and steady," Jack reminded Sam. She rolled her eyes, but it went unseen, lost in the darkness, the only light available coming from the headlights.

Sam's head was still swimming, but she knew it wouldn't go away as long as they were there, and would

likely get worse. "Which way, Mick?" she asked.

They all flicked on their flashlights and followed Mick into the darkness. The mammoth rock in front of them was barely visible against the night sky, but was enough to give them a sense of direction. In the short time Sam and Jack lived in Sedona, they had never stopped to explore the trails near Bell Rock; they would have to rely on Mick's expertise of the area.

"How long until we're at the spot?" Jack asked, checking his watch. *4:45 am.*

"It's only about a thirty-minute hike on the upper trail to the strongest part of the vortex," Mick replied. "There's a small ledge, but barely enough room for two people."

"What direction does it face?" Sam asked. "It needs to face east. The sun needs to hit the egg directly."

"You sure do know your phoenix lore, don't you?" Mick asked rhetorically with a chuckle. Sam wasn't in a joking mood and refused to respond. Mick continued, "Only a tiny part of the ledge faces east, just big enough for the egg to fit. You'll have to prop the egg up against the rock to get it in the right position. The real problem is the winds. They whip around pretty good up there. You'll need to watch your balance and make sure the egg is secured."

Great, Sam thought. *It's always something.* Tommy grabbed Sam's hand and squeezed, letting her know everything would be okay. She squeezed back, appreciating the comfort and support.

As they made their way up the trail, the group had to

stop several times for Sam to rest and regain her composure, each stop a little longer than the previous. The energy pulsated through her body, making her weak and slowing their progress considerably. Soon they were stopping every hundred yards. They were already one hour into the thirty-minute hike, yet barely halfway to their destination.

"Sam, you don't have to do this," Jack worried. "Mick and I can get the egg there if you need to stop." Sunrise was in twenty minutes, and there was no more time to lose.

Sam shot back in anger, "No! No one is doing this but me. Ash needs me, and I will not let him down!"

"Are you sure it's not you who needs Ash?" Mick butted in.

Jack jumped to his daughter's defense. "Completely uncalled for," he scolded.

Mick's quip only motivated Sam. She popped back to her feet and pushed forward at a breakneck pace, Tommy at her heels. "Let's go!" Jack and Mick struggled to keep up.

"Sam, we need to wait for them. We need Mick to guide us to the spot," Tommy requested.

"I know where we need to go." The power of the vortex continued to intensify, causing Sam to wobble in her stride, but she let the energy guide her. If the energy strengthened, she stayed the course; if it began to weaken, she corrected until she felt it raging through her body.

The sky was beginning to lighten to the east. The rocks started coming to life, shedding darkness in favor of the vibrant red hues for which they'd become famous. A low layer of fog filled the valley below, and in the distance, clouds covered the horizon.

Sam looked back, but only Tommy was in sight; her dad and Mick had fallen well behind. With less than five minutes to spare, Sam and Tommy reached the ledge. Seeing it in person, Sam now understood what Mick had explained. The ledge was only three feet wide and four feet long, hugging the rock and coming to a point facing east. The wall of the rock plummeted 500 feet below. The winds swirled in every direction.

Sam could barely move as the power of the vortex dropped her to her knees once again. Tommy pulled the backpack off her shoulders and removed the egg from within, before she crumpled fully to the ground. With Sam in pain and unable to fight off the energy field, Tommy crawled on his belly to the outcrop and positioned Ash upright, carefully balanced. The egg wobbled precariously in the winds. Tommy scurried back and pulled Sam into his lap, and between his legs, cradling her against his chest, his arms wrapped around her torso. They waited.

Jack and Mick finally caught up, watching from the trail below. The sky began to lighten as the minutes passed. "It should've happened by now," Sam weakly muttered, looking up at Tommy worried. They turned their attention back to the egg, which continued to shake dangerously on the ledge. On the horizon, a thick layer of clouds continued to block the sun despite the clear blue skies above. Ash sat there, trapped in the shell.

Sam began to sob. "He's not coming back. Ash is gone forever."

Tommy pulled Sam to her feet and steadied her against the rock. "I'll get him. He should stay with you." He kissed her on the cheek and took a step toward Ash, as a massive gale swept across the rock, the egg tumbling off the cliff edge.

Sam let out a bloodcurdling scream, "No!!!!" Her echoing cries filled the valley as rays of sunlight penetrated the cloudy horizon, blinding them and forcing them to shield their eyes. Sam's shrieks continued to echo, growing seemingly louder, but she hadn't made another sound.

Out of the foggy canyon, a bright light pulsed red and green—the source of the screeching. Sam and Tommy followed the glow as it disappeared behind the backside of Bell Rock. *Could it be?* Sam thought. The lights reappeared and circled back toward them. The fog broke, and a young phoenix rushed past Sam and Tommy, spiraling upward around the rock.

"Ash!" Sam yelled in disbelief. "You're alive!" Tommy joined in the excitement, grabbing and hugging her. Tears of exuberance ran down their faces as they watched the little phoenix swoop in and out of the canyon. He was much smaller than his previous form, roughly the size of a bald eagle.

Below, Jack and Mick hugged and laughed, overjoyed by Ash's rebirth. "I wish you could've had this for Cinder," Jack condoled.

"Me too," replied Mick, wiping away a tear. "But I'm

so glad Sam got her wish. You raised one amazing kiddo. You should be proud." Jack smiled.

Sam could overhear Jack and Mick's conversation in her head despite the distance between them. Her mood turned, and a look of consternation crossed her face. "There's something else I need to do," she told Tommy.

"What are you talking about?" Tommy responded quizzically. Sam stumbled, picked up her backpack, and headed toward the ledge. "Wait, what are you doing?" Tommy followed as closely as possible, seeing she wasn't fully steady on her feet.

"This isn't the strongest part of the vortex. It's up there," Sam said, looking up.

"Sam, you're in no condition. Why do you need to go up there?" Tommy inquired, trying to understand. Sam balanced the backpack on her knee, against the rock. She reached inside and pulled out Cinder's egg.

"You brought Cinder? She's still alive?" Tommy asked.

"Guess it's time to find out." Sam placed the egg safely back in the sack and secured it over her shoulders.

The tiny ledge sat perpendicular to a large vertical crevice in the rock. Sam placed her left hand and right foot into the crack and pulled herself up. Then she switched, right hand and left foot, and pulled herself up even further. Tommy stepped beneath her, ready to follow.

"No, Tommy. I have to do this on my own. I'll be okay, I promise." Sam grabbed her head with her free hand, wincing in pain.

"Sam, please don't do this. We can come back another day when you're feeling better." Tommy begged and pleaded to no avail. "Wait!" he demanded. Sam stopped climbing. Tommy reached into his pocket and revealed the heart-shaped stone Sam had given him at the cave. "For luck," Tommy said, handing her the stone.

"I'll be back," she said, blowing him a kiss. Sam continued her ascent.

Sam scaled the rock for twenty feet before finally pulling herself over another ledge and out of Tommy's view; her dad and Mick also out of sight. The winds howled, fierce as ever, as she surveilled her surroundings. Sam stood on a flat, round platform, approximately ten feet in diameter. The power of the vortex was almost too much to handle, but she pushed through the stinging pain.

The energy continued to intensify as Sam moved toward the center of the span. Then she spied it . . . *A phoenix . . . just like the one on the tree stump . . . and the garage door.* Sam dropped to one knee and pulled the egg from inside the backpack. "Here goes nothing," she proclaimed.

With Cinder in hand, Sam pressed through the force of the vortex until she was standing on the marker. It dropped her to her knees. The pain was more intense than anything she'd ever felt. Her eyes glazed over, like they had at the stump, but this time she was able to maintain some control. She placed the egg on top of the symbol, and it immediately began to glow white-hot. Light began to pulse and shoot from Sam's fingers, then her eyes. She held on tight to the egg, keeping it place, then . . . *FLASH!* It was brighter than the sun and filled the valley. Tommy, Jack, and Mick averted their eyes from the blinding light.

"Sam!" they all yelled repeatedly. The sky returned to normal as the radiance dissipated. "Sam!" they continued to yell without a response except for their echoes from the valley below.

Tommy decided to climb after Sam. Halfway up the fractured rock, a phoenix swooped by him. "Ash! Sam needs our help!" he shouted. He continued as fast as he could until he reached the top. Tommy couldn't believe what he saw next.

Two phoenixes stood over Sam's lifeless body; Ash at her head, Cinder at her feet. They simultaneously pulled their wings over their heads and brought them toward each other, covering Sam underneath. They started to sing. As they did so, their feathers pulsed and flashed myriad colors. They continued for several minutes. Tommy never interrupted, his gaze never leaving Sam's hand and arm, which were peeking out from beneath the birds. He looked for any sign of . . . *her finger twitched.*

Ash and Cinder tucked their wings back into their bodies and hopped back, allowing Tommy to join Sam. She slowly opened her eyes. "Sam! Sam, are you okay?" Tommy pressed.

"Did it work?" she asked faintly.

"See for yourself." Tommy helped Sam sit upright. Ash and Cinder nestled together, cooing and whistling. Sam's eyes widened. She pulled Tommy close with an astonishing

amount of energy for someone who'd just been brought to health. She kissed him hard.

Ash and Cinder took to the skies, circling each other just above the kids, flames dancing from their feathers. Tommy and Sam watched the birds' aerial dance in amazement. Ash looked like a smaller, cuter version of his previous self. Cinder dazzled, mostly yellow, with purples and greens running down her back and into her tail feathers.

"Are you okay to climb back down?" Tommy asked her. Sam nodded, her cheeks still blushing from the kiss. The vortex didn't seem to be affecting her any longer. She could still feel its strength, but she was in control and no longer in pain.

Sam and Tommy made their way carefully down the crack in the rock, Tommy first so he could help Sam keep her balance from below. When they reached the bottom, Jack and Mick were waiting and rushed to their sides.

"Are you okay?" Jack asked. "What happened up there?"

Sam could feel the birds circling above. She looked up and waited for them to catch on.

"Cinder?" Mick exclaimed. "Cinder!!" The little phoenix dove down at the sound of her voice, and perched on her arm. "Oh, my sweet Cinder, I can't believe you're alive." The bird cooed and clicked, pushing her head into the crux of Mick's neck for a cuddle. "How did you . . . ? This is unbelievable."

"It's only make-believe if you don't believe. That's what mom always said," Sam responded, grinning at her dad.

"You made me a believer. Thank you, sweetie. I owe you everything," Mick replied.

Ash joined the group, coming to rest on the ground. Sam, impressed by Mick's handling of Cinder, put out her arm. Ash hopped up and gave Sam a nuzzle of his own.

"Should we head back to the house?" Jack asked. "Maybe some breakfast?"

"Sounds wonderful!" Mick exclaimed.

"Not yet," Sam replied solemnly. Their joy turned dour as she put her forehead to Ash's and closed her eyes. A tear strolled down her cheek.

"Princess?" Jack asked. Sam didn't respond immediately, remaining locked with Ash.

"They can't stay. Ash and Cinder must return to Paradise immediately," she lamented. "We have to say our goodbyes."

With tears welling, Mick turned and walked away from the group. Her bond with Cinder was as strong as ever. She had waited nine years for this moment, and she wanted time alone to say goodbye.

Jack, Sam, and Tommy huddled around Ash to say their farewells. Ash jumped to Jack and pushed his head into his chest and cooed. "Good luck, Ash. Safe travels," said Jack, petting him on the head.

He then leaped to Tommy. "Goodbye, friend. Thank you for everything." The phoenix clicked and whistled his response.

Finally, Ash returned to Sam and placed his head

against hers again. Sam's eyes were overflowing. "I'll never forget you. Thank you." She couldn't get any more words out, as she sobbed uncontrollably. She knew he had to return home, but she couldn't stand the thought of never seeing him again.

Your love is immense, your powers beyond words. May we meet again in Paradise. Only Sam could hear the message—it was meant only for her.

Ash took to the sky; Cinder promptly joined him. One last song filled the valley, a strange, but beautiful melody, never before heard. Within seconds the birds climbed out of view, a small, double flash of light the last visible record of their existence. They were finally on their way home to Paradise.

CHAPTER TWENTY-THREE

Mick pulled Betty up the steep driveway to a creaking stop. As they got out, Charlie, Chris, Eli, and Popcorn were there to greet them. "Welcome back!" Charlie proclaimed. But it became quickly apparent that the reunion would be less than a merry occasion.

Chris rushed to Tommy's side and immediately recognized the redness in his eyes. "What's going on? What happened?" The melancholy led Chris to fear the worst. "Did you get there in time?"

"Yes, son," Jack replied for the group.

"Why the long faces? Where's Ash?" he pressed, expecting the bird to swoop from the sky and join them at any moment.

"He's gone," Sam explained. "Back to Paradise. He couldn't stay. I'm sorry you couldn't say goodbye."

They all shuffled into Mick's house and plopped down on the couches, exasperated from the morning's events. Jack introduced Charlie and the boys to Mick and told the story of

their river trip, the cabin, the stolen Jeep, and his run-in with the law.

"Anybody hungry?" Mick asked.

Everyone turned to Eli and Popcorn, waiting for a response. The latter answered Mick with a raised paw. "What?" Eli asked, intimidated by being put on the spot. Sam laughed, breaking the somber mood, allowing everybody else to join in the much-needed relief.

"Well, Lunchbox?" Chris asked. Eli's tummy grumbled loudly, giving everyone the answer. They couldn't contain their laughter. Mick withdrew to the kitchen to start cooking, allowing them to continue catching up.

Sam picked up where Jack had left off, backtracking a bit to explain how she came upon Cinder's egg, how Ash's egg grew and transformed, and the vortex in the backyard. "After breakfast, I'll take you and show you," Sam offered.

"Are you sure about that, Princess?" Jack asked. "Maybe you should rest a bit. You've been through so much in the last few days."

Sam rolled her eyes loudly, "It's okay, Dad. Something happened up there on Bell Rock. It doesn't hurt anymore."

Sam continued with the story and Tommy's bravery, ensuring Ash's egg was in place at sunrise, and how he was there for her after the phoenixes healed her. Tommy was worried that she'd tell the story of their first real kiss, but Sam spared him the embarrassment, keeping their secret safe. It didn't keep Tommy from blushing at the memory, but no one noticed except Sam. Charlie was proud of his boy and how he'd responded and grown in the last week, with all he had endured. Chris, sitting closest to Tommy, messed his hair as a proud big brother.

"Soup's on!" Mick yelled from the kitchen.

"Soup for breakfast?" Eli questioned. They all laughed, confusing Eli even more.

"And no critters at the table, please," she continued. Popcorn lamented the lack of acceptance with an aggressive wag of the tail, but remained by Eli's side, hopeful some under-the-table scraps were coming his way.

"Let's go, kiddo," Charlie said, putting an arm around Eli and pulling him toward the kitchen.

Mick had prepared quite a spread with eggs, bacon, hash browns, fresh fruit, sourdough toast, and an assortment of jams and jellies. They ate well that morning, enjoying the food and the company. Laughs abounded, and a low din was palpable with several conversations going at the same time. It felt like family and Sam couldn't help but look around, appreciative of every person in the room and what they meant to her. It was her own personal Thanksgiving.

After breakfast, Sam was eager to show off her newfound powers to everybody. "Can we wait a few? Maybe let our food settle?" Jack asked his daughter. "And don't roll your eyes." Sam couldn't help it; eye-rolling was second nature at this point. Jack shook his head and laughed it off.

As the morning waned into afternoon, the group made their way to the backyard and settled into a circle of chairs around an open-pit bonfire. The weather was in the upper

sixties so the fire wasn't needed, but it was perfect post-feast relaxation.

The kids were anxious to get back to the stump and started to inch their way closer, first playing on the lawn near the house, then making their way to the corral, to pet the horses. Popcorn was curious about Mick's equine companions, sniffing around their hooves and dodging their annoyed stomps. Jack, Charlie, and Mick didn't budge from their seats, letting the kids know it wasn't quite time for show-and-tell.

"Those kids have ants in their pants," chuckled Mick. "Can't say I blame them though, especially Sam. Once I learned I had a gift, I was out there for hours trying to figure it out."

"Yeah, she's just like her mother. She feels that glimmer of magic and can't help herself," Jack responded.

"Like her mother?" Mick asked. "She has powers too?"

"She did," Jack offered with a dour smile. "Sam is every bit her mother's daughter."

Mick's mood quickly dampened at the realization. "Did? Oh, Jack, I'm so sorry. How long has it been, if you don't mind my asking?"

"Eighteen months. And not a day goes by that I wish I could bring her back and see her again. Sam's struggled since her mom's been gone. This trip was the first time I've seen her come out of her shell. I'm not sure what to do with her now. She never knew of her mom's powers. I feel like if I tell her, it'll put her right back into her funk."

Mick did her best to comfort Jack. "Well, your secret is safe with me. You'll tell her when the time is right, but know that she's stronger than you think. Trust in her, and she'll return it ten-fold." Jack nodded his appreciation.

"Nan was some woman, Jack. You never were good enough for her," Charlie reminisced with a hardy laugh. "I'm not sure anyone would have been."

"You got that right," Jack said, eking out a smile. He turned to Mick, "I should probably tell her sooner than later, I suppose. There's a lot she doesn't know about her mom, but I think it may finally be time. Nan left her a gift that I'm not supposed to give to Sam until she turns sixteen, but I think maybe she's ready for it."

"Well, you have my attention," Mick exclaimed.

"Mine too, buddy," Charlie said inquisitively. "You've been holding out on me for years." He turned to Mick, "He's been dangling this carrot for as long as I can remember, but he's never been willing to tell me."

"You need to promise not to say anything to Sam before I can talk to her." Charlie and Mick nodded in compliance. "There's a reason I call Sam 'Princess'. Nan was the daughter of a Tahltan chieftain in British Columbia. She was quite literally royalty . . . as is Sam."

Charlie and Mick listened as Jack explained more about Nan's background, how their culture passed through the mother, and how her grandfather helped bring the different clans under one rule. Sam had never met her grandparents, or Nan's brother and cousins, who lived there. Jack hoped to

take her there soon, so she could meet them and learn about her heritage. Sam only knew that her mom was from Canada and had moved to Seattle for college. Outside of a few tales of indigenous folklore, Sam didn't know much about that side of her family tree.

"You're saying Sam is an actual princess, and she doesn't know?" questioned Charlie. "Why didn't Nan want her to know?"

"She wanted her to have a normal childhood, without that type of pressure. She didn't want it to go to her head, and wanted to make sure Sam was mature enough to handle the responsibility. Not that she would have any responsibilities as a princess, but just that she wouldn't become too big for her own britches."

"Is that the 'gift?'" Mick asked. "Or is there something else?"

"There's something else, but I think I've said too much already. You'll see soon enough."

"Seriously?" Charlie laughed in disbelief. "You're killing me, Jack."

"What's that about curiosity and a cat?" Mick replied slyly. "I can't wait to find out. I'm sure it'll be a wonderful surprise for her."

Jack refused to reveal any more clues or information. He stood and started walking toward the corral, to join the kids and let Sam know it was time to show off her powers to the others. Charlie and Mick followed.

"Ready, Princess?" Jack asked as he arrived. Charlie

and Mick grinned at one another and the insider information they possessed.

"Beyond ready!" Sam exclaimed, jumping down from the bars of the corral.

As they meandered through the trees toward the stump, Sam's head began to tingle, causing her to press her fingers against her temples. Mick took notice. "Push through," she encouraged. "You got this."

Sam shook it off and pressed forward, trying to take her mind off the dull pain. "Did you paint the phoenix on the garage yourself?" she asked Mick.

"Sure did, little lady. Once I saw the mark on the stump, I couldn't help myself. I'm not much of an artist, but I'm proud of it."

"You should be," Jack replied. It's really great." He smiled at Mick, blushing ever so slightly. He was finding himself enamored with her wit and her passion. The feelings were new, and something he hadn't felt since Nan's passing. He felt guilty, but Sam helped break him from the thought.

"When I was on top of Bell Rock with Cinder, the same symbol was there. I think it's a landmark for them, so they know where to go. It was the most powerful part of the vortex."

"What about at the clearing? The boulder had the heart on it, not a phoenix," Charlie pondered.

"That's right, and at the entrance to the cave, too," added Jack.

"There was a heart at the cave? I don't remember that,"

offered Tommy.

"It showed up when Dad and I went back for Ash's remains . . . when we found the baby worm. It allowed us to pass through without getting wet from the waterfall," Sam said, trying to put the pieces of the puzzle together. "But, it disappeared after we left the cave the last time."

"Maybe it was inside the cave and we missed it," Chris offered.

"Maybe," Sam replied, still contemplating.

Jack believed he had an answer or at least a partial one, but he wouldn't reveal his thought until he could give Sam her gift, away from the others, when he could explain everything.

As they approached the stump, Sam could feel the energy through her entire body. Tommy was by her side, ready to catch her if needed. "Are you ready, Sam?" Mick asked. Sam looked to Tommy for assurance; he kissed her on the cheek. She then looked to her dad, who nodded. "Always believe in yourself," Mick continued. "You control the energy. You're in charge . . . no pun intended." The line got a chuckle from Jack and Charlie.

Sam stepped up onto the stump and immediately dropped to one knee. The winds picked up and her eyes glowed blue as sparks jumped from her fingers. "Believe, Princess," encouraged Jack.

Slowly, Sam pushed herself up and back on both feet. Light poured from her fingers down to the ground, then up into the swirling winds. Everyone encircled her and watched in awe as Sam raised her head and turned her palms skyward, fire now filling her hands. She was in complete control.

Only days earlier, Sam had been a relatively normal twelve-year-old girl, but she had transformed. Reborn from her grief and in memory of her mother, the words never rang truer . . .

It's only make-believe if you don't believe.

Joel Thomas Feldman is a husband, father, military veteran, engineer, and author. With a bachelor's degree in TV/Film, and master's in Strategic Intelligence, Joel has spent his career working in and around the U.S. Air Force. Now, after 20+ years, he has returned to his true passion of writing, with the first book in his Journeys of the Immortal series. Joel lives in Southern California with his wife, Michaela; and their two children, Jack and Thais.

Learn more about the author at:

Joelthomasfeldman.com
Instagram.com/joelthomasfeldman

Printed in Great Britain
by Amazon

49387238R00142